D1589440

MAR 2020

2000670663

RENEGADE'S LEGACY

The mystery man rode into town the day that they buried Big Al McCord. Some people suspected he was 'Dan McCord', a runaway kid returning after twenty years — and out for vengeance. His arrival shook the townsfolk, bringing turmoil and gunsmoke to the rangeland, panicking the corrupt officials and folk with a bad conscience. But Brett had his own agenda — and when they found out what it was, that part of Dakota would never be the same again.

Books by Rick Dalmas
in the Linford Western Library:

SIX FOR LARAMIE

RICK DALMAS

RENEGADE'S LEGACY

Complete and Unabridged

LINFORD
Leicester

First published in Great Britain in 2010 by
Robert Hale Limited
London

First Linford Edition
published 2011
by arrangement with
Robert Hale Limited
London

British Library CIP Data

Dalmas, Rick.
　Renegade's legacy. - -
　(Linford western library)
　1. Western stories.
　2. Large type books.
　I. Title II. Series
　823.9'2–dc22

ISBN 978–1–4448–0840–7

Published by
F. A. Thorpe (Publishing)
Anstey, Leicestershire

Set by Words & Graphics Ltd.
Anstey, Leicestershire
Printed and bound in Great Britain by
T. J. International Ltd., Padstow, Cornwall

This book is printed on acid-free paper

1

Who Dies this Day?

He heard the singing as he rode the straw-maned roan into town, entering by the south end of the main drag.

Many voices were raised in the solemn cadences of a hymn, coming from a white-painted clapboard building the size of a small hall. It had a steeply pitched shingle roof — there were heavy snowfalls up here in winter — but no tower. Must be the local church, though; he could see the wooden cross nailed above the closed doors now.

It wasn't Sunday, it was Tuesday by his count, though it could be Wednesday — in any case, a weekday, so it must be some kind of a special service. Christening, maybe. Wedding? Funeral?

He recognized the hymn: 'Rock Of Ages', so it most likely was a funeral.

By now he had ridden far enough to see the edge of a small cemetery around one side of the church. There was freshly turned earth of an open grave amongst the headstones.

Yeah, funeral, right enough. But whose? Who had died this day? The very day of his arrival. Was that some kind of an omen? He knew plenty of men — and women — who would consider it so. It didn't bother him either way.

Whoever had died had missed a fine day — the golden light of afternoon under the bluest thing God had ever made: the vault of a cloudless North Dakota sky.

He was far enough into Main now to see that the wide street was deserted, except for patient mounts drooping at various hitchrails, both sides. The stores and saloons were closed. A pariah dog rummaged in a pile of trash in the mouth of an alley, whining hungrily;

otherwise it looked like a ghost town.

The dead person must have been someone mighty important to close down the entire town for a day.

The entrance to Dowd's Livery — expanded some, it seemed to him — was still doorless and he turned the roan into the aisle, chose an empty stall halfway along on the west side. He off-saddled, gave the horse a quick affectionate rub behind the right ear, then got it a nosebag of oats from a bin.

He took down currycomb and brush from a narrow shelf across the rear of the stall and hummed tunelessly to himself as he groomed the mount. It chomped contentedly, its dusty coat twitching in pleasure as the brush passed over its withers.

Then there was a metallic *click*! behind him and a harsh, wheezy voice demanded, 'What the hell you doin' in that stall?'

The fat man standing in the aisle just outside the stall got out only part of his query, then leapt back as the stranger

3

dropped currycomb and brush, whirling as he went down to one knee, the six-gun that had been holstered on his right side somehow magically appearing in his hand, hammer cocked.

'Judas priest!' gasped the fat livery man, dropping the pair of polished spurs he had been holding. They clinked as they hit the soggy ground by his feet — just like a gun hammer cocking. He raised his pudgy hands quickly to shoulder level, his moon face a ghastly yellow, mouth sagging, eyes bulging. 'T-take it easy, mister! Din' mean to startle you! Was just my spur rowels clinkin' . . . '

The stranger rose smoothly to his feet, long-muscle easy, clear blue eyes the colour of rim ice on a mountain stream checking the aisle behind the livery man. Only then did he lower the Colt's hammer and return the gun to his holster, but he kept his hand on the cedar butt.

'What's it look like I'm doing?'

The fat man licked his lips. 'I-I guess

4

you're currycombin' your bronc. But my sign at the entrance says to check with the office first before goin' to a stall.'

'Never noticed. Did I pick a stall that's reserved?'

'No-ooo. It's just that it's one of my rules.'

'You big on rules, friend?'

The reasonable query seemed to calm the fat man some. 'I make 'em, I like 'em obeyed. Say, I know you?'

He was squinting now, looking up into the face of the lean and rangy six-footer standing beside the still feeding roan. It was a tough face, well-used over what the fat man guessed would be about thirty-some years, pushing towards the forty mark. There was a nest of scars above the left eye, like a man earns in a fight, an injury that had been busted open several times after the original wound had long healed over. Another scar bisected the left cheek, angled, straight and thin — the kind left by a

5

razor-sharp blade. The mouth was wide, kind of thin-lipped, and looked like it wouldn't smile a hell of a lot. The jaw — well, the jaw was square-cut, like a piece of four-by-two hardwood, fringed by a three-day stubble, sprinkled here and there with a strand of silver.

Yeah — closer to forty than thirty.

'Had your look?'

The stableman started. 'Er — sorry. Thought I recognized you, but guess I was wrong. I'm Phil Rowley. This is my livery.'

'What happened to Burt Dowd?'

Rowley's eyes pinched down a little. 'Retired to Cheyenne. You been here before if you recollect Burt Dowd.'

'You must be the only one not at the funeral.'

Rowley's flabby mouth tightened and his pulpy nose appeared to twitch a little, surprising the stranger, who carefully hadn't answered the question or given his name.

'I was never impressed by Al McCord. Never give me a lot of

6

business, always told his riders to leave their mounts at the hitchrails, do their business, then get back to his spread. Skinflint! He mighta run things when he was alive, but he ain't runnin' me now he's dead. That's why I'm here and not at the graveside.'

He broke off as he saw those ice-blue eyes narrow, the wide shoulders tense. 'McCord? That's who's dead?'

Rowley nodded, looking more closely at this newcomer. 'Yeah. Guess someone finally had a gutful of his rawhidin' ways, shot him in the back couple days ago, out on the Lowery Canyon trail.' He paused, cleared his throat. 'If you come in by the south, you'd've come up the Lowery, wouldn't you?'

'No business of yours. *Damn!* Looks like I arrived a few days too late.' He seemed to be talking for his own benefit.

'You was comin' to see McCord?'

'How much I owe you for using your stall? I'll leave my horse here — overnight, at least.'

7

'Well, I hire out full day or part thereof. Just the one price . . . a dollar.'

'No wonder you're so fat. You must eat pretty damn good, charging those prices.'

Rowley looked indignant but didn't get a chance to speak. The other took a coin from his pocket and flicked it at the livery man, who deftly caught it — lots of practice.

'No roomin' houses open,' he volunteered, 'not till after sundown. But the Redbird about halfway down the next block is pretty good. They don't mind you helpin' yourself to an empty room if there's no one behind the counter. Just sign in, pick a key from the board an' go on up.'

The stranger looked a mite leery at this sudden helpful advice, then nodded, picked up his warbag in his left hand. He slid his Winchester rifle from the saddle scabbard with his right, pushing past Rowley in the aisle. 'Keep an eye on my saddle.'

'Sheriff don't allow folk to walk our

8

streets with naked guns, Mister — er — ? Din' catch your name . . . '

'He at the funeral?'

Rowley looked piqued, nodded jerkily. 'Yeah. He'd be sure to pay his respects to the McCords.'

'Still McCords living round here then?'

'Hell, yeah! Big Al's brats, Dean and Belle, out at the Arrowhead — their ranch.'

'Yeah, I know — ' The man cut it short, nodded and went on out.

In the sunshine he glanced down towards the church. The congregation had moved out to the little cemetery now, gathered around the open grave. Metal handles on a polished wooden coffin caught and reflected the rays of the westering sun, brief bright flashes between the legs of the mourners.

'Just too damn late!' he muttered with feeling.

He turned and strolled across the street towards a paint-faded sign that said:

9

Redbird Rooms
Clean sheets, wholesome food.
70 cents a night. 40 cents room only.

That sounded all right to him and he opened the half-glass door and stepped into an empty lobby.

He hoped Rowley was right about self-service if no one was around. He made for the untended counter and the board with several keys hanging on it behind. He took Number 9.

* * *

He was shaving, his face reflected in an oval mirror above the washstand, when there was a knock on the door. He paused, scraped the razor in two short swipes over his upper lip, then wiped his face with the towel as there was another knock, louder this time, more impatient.

He was still wearing his gunbelt, though he was shirtless. He eased the Colt out, hammer spur under his

10

thumb as he crossed the worn carpet and reached for the door with his left hand.

There was a tall woman standing there and she looked as if she had a deal of Indian blood in her. Dusky-gold skin, slightly slanted, very dark eyes, gleaming straight black hair pulled back from a face with barely prominent cheekbones. The lips were full and deep red. Hard to guess her age — maybe thirty, late twenties, thereabouts.

He nodded curtly and the dark eyes followed his movement as he holstered the Colt. 'You'd be Miss Redbird?'

'I am Raina Redbird. I don't know your name because you didn't sign the register.' Her voice was neither friendly nor hostile and her gaze was steady.

'Figured to do it after I cleaned up.' He looked at her dark-grey blouse with embroidered native flowers on the collar and over her left breast; she also had on a muted-blue silk neckerchief with a silver clasp, a wide buckskin belt with an oval silver buckle and a dark

11

brown skirt. She was wearing soft buckskin half-boots.

'I was at the funeral, of course, as were my staff. Would you like to come and sign my register now, Mr . . . ?'

'Brett.'

She arched her scant curved eyebrows.

'I'll get my shirt.'

She stood there as he turned away and her eyes narrowed as she saw a few faded criss-crossed scars high up on his white back. Someone had taken a whip to him long ago, she told herself and turned to start down the stairs.

At the counter in the foyer, where a male clerk was now sorting mail, she turned the register and looked at the name he had printed in block letters. Her eyes sought his sober, newly shaved face.

'Just 'Brett'? I mean, is that your surname, or your first name?'

'Does for both.'

Her gaze lingered, then she nodded and set the register back in its place on the counter. 'Will you be having your meals here, Mr — Brett?'

'Just Brett — and yeah, I guess so.' He was digging in his pocket as he spoke, sorted through a handful of coins. 'I'll be here at least a couple of nights.'

'Then that'll be one dollar and forty cents, thank you.' There was a faint accent there that he found pleasant enough. He was still trying to get used to a half-breed Indian woman running a boarding house in a frontier town. It sure wasn't usual, but she had the look of an independent spirit about her, so he guessed she was tolerably successful, though the rooming house was no palace.

He paid, aware of the clerk watching him surreptitiously, and started to turn away from the counter when Phil Rowley came in followed by a tall, well-built man with a black moustache and wearing a sheriff's star.

Raina Redbird was possibly the only one in the foyer who noticed how the

13

sun-faded material of Brett's blue shirt stretched across his shoulders as his muscles tensed.

Rowley pointed. 'That's him, Sheriff. Dunno his name. Din' seem to want to give it.'

The sheriff hooked his thumbs in his slanting gunbelt, cocked his head slightly. He had a triangular face, not unhandsome, but weak-chinned, and the lips beneath the moustache seemed kind of thin to Brett. He ignored the woman.

'You walked through my town carrying a naked rifle,' the lawman accused.

'That so?'

The lawman frowned and Raina Redbird went very still. The sheriff jerked his head slightly towards the livery man. 'That's what Phil says.'

'Ah. Our upstanding, law-abiding livery owner,' Brett said, staring hard at Rowley. 'S'pose I call him a liar?'

Breath hissed audibly through the clerk's buck teeth. The woman grew an inch as she tensed, and Rowley paled.

14

Only the sheriff showed no emotion.

'Sound like fightin' words to me.' Brett shrugged and the lawman swivelled grey eyes to the livery man. 'What you say to that, Phil?'

'I say I saw him! He left my stables carryin' a Winchester without a scabbard! He coulda slid it back in the scabbard after I warned him he was breakin' the law . . . '

'Ordinance, Phil. Town ordinance. Phil's right, mister. It's about time you had a name.'

Brett told him and Rowley frowned. 'Brett what?'

'Just Brett.'

Rowley leaned towards the sheriff and said quietly, a little breathlessly, 'That was Molly McCord's maiden name! Knew he was tryin' to hide somethin', not comin' clean about his name.'

There was a sudden stillness in the foyer and Brett frowned. 'Who's Molly McCord?'

'You seemed to know the McCord

name when I told you was Al bein' buried!' Rowley said smugly.

'Most folk've heard of him, even outside the Territories.'

'Never mind!' snapped the lawman. 'I'm Barton Gill, and I don't allow unsheathed guns on my streets.'

'They were deserted, so I wasn't exactly endangering anyone's life, Sheriff. If this lard-belly is your only witness, it comes down to his word against mine, right?'

Barton Gill smiled crookedly, without mirth. 'Seein' as I don't know you, I'd have to take Phil's word.'

'All right. What's the penalty?'

'Five dollar fine. Or you want to fuss about it, I could jail you.'

Gill bored his grey eyes into Brett who smiled faintly. 'Reckon not.'

Gill frowned, paler now. 'Why you pushin' this?'

'Ah, the hell with it. OK, Sheriff, I won't do it again. That all right?'

'No it ain't all right!' Gill snapped. 'You're all together too damn sassy for

16

my likin', Brett. You ain't welcome here. You pay the fine and you can stay overnight, while I check my Wanted dodgers. So mebbe I'll put you in a cell to make sure you're on hand should I find one that — '

Barton Gill had been standing side-on for the last couple of minutes and suddenly his right hand appeared, across his body, holding his six-gun, pointed at Brett.

But he froze, staring dully at the cocked Colt held rock-steady, barrel aligned on the centre of his chest.

'God almighty!' breathed Rowley. 'He — he did a fast draw back at my livery, too, Bart! He's a damn gun-fighter!'

'You got the look, Brett.' Gill hadn't lowered his gun but the tip of his tongue wet his lips. 'You don't pull a gun on me in my town, mister.'

'Then don't pull one on me. You won't find any dodgers on me, Sheriff. I aim to stick around for a spell. You've got my word I'll be here in the

17

morning. That good enough?'

'Not by a damn sight!' But Gill didn't push it: it was clearly dangerous to question this hard man's word right now. 'I'll take it — for the moment, after you pay me five dollars. But you and me ain't finished, Brett. Not by a damn sight!'

Then Brett said a strange thing, unsmiling.

'I know that, Sheriff. Thing is, I ain't finished with this town, *not by a damn sight*, neither. So you don't need to worry none about my leaving, 'cause I don't aim to, not for quite some time.'

2

Man about Town

The Indian woman was helping a waitress clear the long eating table on one side of the big dining room. There had been almost a dozen men and one boy at the table with Brett at supper; all seemed to enjoy their hearty meal.

Alone now, he rolled a cigarette and lounged back in his chair as he lit up. The others had drifted away and the smoke was more than halfway finished when Raina came back from the kitchen.

'There's a balcony runs along the front of the building past your room. Most guests enjoy their after-meal cigarettes up there or in the foyer. You can get a fine view of the Whetstones on a clear day from that balcony, too.'

He looked at the almost finished

cigarette, lifted a boot across his knee and ground the butt against the run-over heel. 'Sorry. Not used to decent company. Round-ups, bunk-houses, line camps and chuck wagons are more my style.'

She smiled faintly. 'It doesn't really matter. You're the only one left at the table. I shouldn't have said anything.' A mite touchy: must still have a hard time of it, now and then. 'Meal to your satisfaction?'

'Real elegant, ma'am. First roast pork I've had in years — and the best.'

She straightened a little and he frowned slightly. What had he said?

She told him, quietly and evenly. 'I'm glad you liked the meal, but I'd like it if you didn't call me 'ma'am'.' He stared blankly and she looked mildly embarrassed. 'It's — I don't quite know how to explain it, but my mother was always called 'ma'am' by the cowboys on our ranch. Because she was married to an Indian, they always managed to make it sound like some sort of dirty joke. 'Yes, *ma'am*!' — 'Whatever you say, *ma'am*!' Oh, maybe I imagined their mockery, but if I did, my mother did, too. She never liked it, though my father thought it fitting: it pleased him to hear his men show her what he took for respect. He was a good man, a gentle man, and he dearly wanted to be accepted by the whites. He thought that owning a small ranch, employing white cowboys and having them speak decently to my mother and me . . . ' She shrugged, and he saw her eyes glistening. *Emotional thoughts cutting loose.*

'He was well ahead of his time. How many Indians d'you know even now who own a ranch — or even a section of land they can call theirs?'

'Yeah, hard for a 'breed, all right.'

She tilted her chin at him. 'My father was a full-blood Lakota. A minor chief in his own land. How d'you feel about such things, anyway?'

He shrugged. 'A man's a man. I take him as I find him. I don't care what colour his skin is. I've knowed some skulking redskins in my day — and I've knowed some I'd ride the river with an' come a hundred miles to do it. Then, I've knowed some miserable whites I wouldn't spit on if they were on fire — as well as some I'd gladly kill for.'

He saw her frown deepen slightly and he chopped off his next words, realizing he had allowed too much emotion to enter his voice. He tried to make little of it, although it was obvious she had noticed.

'No doubt 'breeds and white-eyes say the same sort of things about me and other whites; we all see folk with different eyes. I apologize if I offended you. What do I call you? Miss Redbird?'

Flushing slightly, she shook her head. 'Raina is fine. And an apology isn't necessary.' Then she made an obvious effort to change the subject. 'I rather get the feeling you know this town a lot better than you want people to believe. If I'm prying, just tell me and I'll — '

'Yeah, I guess it could be called

'prying',' he said and saw at once by the way she blinked and took a half-step back that he had surprised her; she hadn't been expecting that answer. He spread his calloused hands innocently. 'You said to — '

'Yes, I asked for that. Well, if there's nothing else you want, Mr Brett, I'd like to close up the dining room for the night.'

'Sure.' He stood, took his hat from the wall peg and placed it on his head. 'I hope the same cook's on duty for breakfast.'

She gave him a faint smile. 'I usually am.'

His turn to show surprise.

'You work mighty hard.' He started to move towards the door, then turned back. 'Bob Dalby still around? He used to be a stock agent . . . '

'I've heard the name but I don't know much about stock agents. There are some offices near the stage depot that deal with that sort of thing — cattle, horses, freight. In the second street on the north side. It parallels Main.'

'That'd be Blackwood?'

'Ye-es. You do seem quite familiar with this town.'

'Studied a map before I came,' he answered curtly, touched two fingers to his hat brim and and strode out of the room.

She began to lift the stained table-cloth, looking after him, as she folded it slowly.

Why did she feel so tense in his presence? It was almost as if there was something to fear about him.

'A strange, hard man,' she murmured quietly.

★ ★ ★

It wasn't much of a balcony, only about three planks wide, just enough to take a chair and allow a man to squeeze into it, lift his feet up to the rails.

He was dressed in a dark shirt — bottle green, actually, and dark-brown corduroy trousers. He took off his

24

pale-blue neckerchief, buttoned his collar, looked down at his sun-bleached hat, curlbrim and battered from much wear. It might show as a pale blur in the darkness but he had better wear it. A man without a hat on the street this time of night would cause more interest than he wanted.

The town seemed to be mostly asleep. There were a couple of tinny pianos playing in the saloons, one accompanying a woman with a reasonable voice as she sang some ballad he didn't know by name, only the tune. A couple of cowboys meandered down the boardwalk, harmless, carrying just enough liquor to make them merry. A rider went past, going like the wind, and a buckboard creaked and rattled down the block. A dog barked, was answered by another, and that brought in a third. Someone hawked and spat. A cat miaowed.

The sounds of a sleeping, law-abiding Western town.

Which meant there might be a town

patrol to make sure things stayed peaceful.

Brett checked his six-gun's loads, the well-oiled cylinder making soft whirring clicks as he turned it, felt for cartridges, chamber by chamber.

He holstered the weapon, set his hat on his head, eased the window up a little more and swung a leg over the sill. His door was locked, the room in darkness, his warbag bunched under the sheets to vaguely resemble a sleeping body, should anyone stare in the window. He had checked from the outside earlier and knew that the second awning post past the corner of the rooming house at the edge of an alley was the best one to use to reach the street. He walked softly, in his socks, carrying his boots in his left hand. When he reached the end of the balcony he tugged them back on, climbed over the shaky rail and lowered himself until his groping feet touched the post.

He wrapped his legs around and

lowered himself down, hand over hand. There was just enough reflected light in the alley for him to see some old paint had flaked off and marked the inside of his trouser legs.

Something to remember when he returned . . .

He brushed it off briefly, tugged on his boots, then slipped down the alley. Keeping to the shadow of the building, he came out into a wider lane that connected to Main at one end and Blackwood at the other.

There were lights burning in Wells Fargo's office and he guessed a late stage must be due. The lamps were turned low so he figured it wouldn't be here for a spell; likely the duty clerk was sleeping at the rear of the depot.

He moved up and down the street, was glad to find Bob Dalby's place on the other side and several buildings along. It was good and dark up here. He smelled hot coke and seared leather: a blacksmith's forge, banked for the night. Yeah, there was the glow showing through a crack in the plank wall. This end of the street was very dark. *Good!*

Dalby had a varnished sign beside his door: *Stock Agent — Robert L. Dalby*. Under the name was written in gold leaf: *Best stock from the best agent!*

'A downright lie, Bob,' Brett said to himself, 'So I guess you ain't changed any.'

The door was locked and the one at the rear had a chain and padlock. He went to the forge, easily loosened a vertical wall plank and ducked inside. The glow from the banked coals showed him the blacksmith's tools on a bench and he chose a short prise. He went back and twisted the padlock free of the chain. He closed the door behind him as he groped down a short hall, smelling musty paper and stale tobacco. He struck a match; squinting quickly he saw he was in a store room. Beyond were two offices, one bigger than the other. The big one had a triangular name plate on the edge of the desk. *Robert L. Dalby* again.

28

'Sure like to see your own name, Bob.'

He lit an oil lamp, kept it turned low, using his body to shield any light that might reach the window, which had a shade pulled down, anyway. He sat in Dalby's padded chair and within ten minutes knew the man was much more successful than he had been fifteen years ago. He wondered whether Dalby was still crooked?

'Hell, yeah! The Bob Dalbys of this world don't change. If they find an easy way to make a dollar, they'll beat it to death before they give up.' He stood slowly. 'Well, Bob, old pard, I'm glad you're such a success; means you got more to lose — and if you was to lose all these records — well, reckon that'd make you tear your hair. You son of a bitch!'

He wrenched open the drawers, pulled out all the papers and threw them in a pile in the kneehole of the desk. Then he turned up the lamp as high as it would go and smashed it on the floor beside the pile.

29

Hot oil spewed out, flames flared instantly. The desk was a bonfire when he slipped into the smaller office, overturned a standing wooden file cabinet, spilling all the ledgers and files and papers on the floor. A single match was enough to start the second bonfire.

Blasting heat made him fling an arm across his face as he hurried back down the passage to the storeroom, where the stacks of many years' files and paperwork walled him in. A small bunch of matches, fired simultaneously, set the blaze going and then he was outside and heading for the shadows.

The dusty windows were already outlined by the consuming fire inside. Glass cracked, shattered. Flames licked outside at the weatherbeaten clapboards and took hold immediately.

Satisfied that the building would be destroyed before the town fire pump could do much more good than a dog lifting its leg, he dodged his way back to the end of the alley running alongside the rooming house.

He was about to step out and make for the balcony post when he heard running boots and a man panted.

'I tell you I smell smoke. Judas Priest! Told you there must be a fire! Look at that!'

Goddamn the luck! The town patrol!

And one of the men had seen him in the spreading glow. 'Hey, you! Hold up, you sonuver!'

Brett moved like a wolf as the man's gun came up — he saw it was a sawed-off shotgun. He disappeared into the shadows as the gun thundered and buckshot screeched off a wall.

'Christ, don't stand there! Go get help!' the deputy yelled at his slow-moving companion. He shucked smoking shells from the shotgun's breech and thumbed in fresh loads.

He ran forward, skirting the shadows where Brett had disappeared. There was a clatter as something was kicked over — or something was thrown to make a man *think* that. In any case, it worked, for the shotgun blasted again, but just one barrel this time, and way off to the left of Brett's position.

The next shot was closer; he winced as a ricocheting ball seared into his left tricep. He flung the second rock he had picked up — at the deputy. The man grunted. The other deputy had run off shouting for help. The roof of Dalby's building collapsed, a volcano of sparks and blazing slivers erupting.

'Hurry up with that fire pump!' the deputy yelled hoarsely, crouching as he tried to stalk Brett. 'Whole damn town'll go up!'

Fire always caused a mighty panic in a timber-built town.

Brett eased back into the wall's shadow and suddenly felt the rough planks of the smithy behind him. He smelled the banked fire inside even above the woodsmoke from Dalby's, as his fingers touched the plank he had loosened earlier. He slid it aside and stepped in. Outside he could hear a lot of voices shouting now and the clatter of a wheeled fire pump being manhandled.

'Get that pump workin'!' shouted the shotgunner. 'I'm goin' after that son of a bitch we seen. Spanner! Skeets! Lend a hand!'

Brett swore silently; he was trapped in here. Then he shucked a handful of cartridges from his belt loops, dumped them on to the glowing coals of the forge, pumped the bellows three swift times. The leather squeaked but he figured it wouldn't be heard over all the racket outside.

'Spread out, two men each side of the street.'

Damn! There must be at least four helping the shotgunner . . .

He was on the far side of the smithy now and found a door with an inside latch. In moments he was outside, in a weed-grown lot that backed on to another backstreet. But all the activity was around the fire now, and . . .

The cartridges began exploding — randomly, two or three close together, singly, rattling in a volley . . .

33

'They must've got him! Down by the blacksmith's!'

Brett moved into the other backstreet away from all the shouting and the thunder of the flames and crashing timbers.

★ ★ ★

He was under the sheets, in his underwear, hair tousled, when there was an urgent hammering on his door.

'Open up in there! Come on! Every man's needed to save the town!'

Squinting, stumbling, he fumbled the door open and stood there blinking sleepily at a sweating townsman who was moving to the next door along. He held a hand over the small blood spot from where the piece of buckshot had broken the skin. 'What the hell . . . ?'

'Grab your boots an' hat, feller! We got us a fire an' we don't get it under control the whole blamed town's gonna go up in smoke!'

'Hell, I'm no firefighter,' Brett said,

34

slurring his voice as if still only half-awake.

'You are tonight!' The townsman kicked and beat on the door of the next room. 'Come on! Drop your cocks an' grab your socks, you fellers! Leave them whores an' *get out here*!'

It was an exciting night.

Brett joined the long line of the bucket brigade, passing slopping pails from hand to hand. The old manual fire pump was of little use and by the time the fire died down, two buildings were nothing more than a pile of hissing, stinking ashes and two more were badly scorched. Bob Dalby's place was totally destroyed.

3

Suspect

Brett was at the washbench behind the rooming house, rinsing his undershirt which was slightly bloodstained and had a small rip in the cloth where the buckshot pellet had penetrated. His arm was stiff and sore to touch — mostly, he reckoned, from working the bucket line last night, but the small wound seemed red and a trifle swollen.

He had dug out the misshapen pellet and flicked it out the window, but he knew he needed iodine or some antiseptic to make sure infection didn't set in.

'I'll do your washing for you. It's included in the price and I boil up bed clothes every day.'

Brett snapped his head up as Raina appeared. She was holding a shallow basket of corn, being on her way to the chicken pens. He couldn't hide the blood-tinged water in the bowl, although most of the stain had come out of the undershirt. She frowned slightly.

'Have you hurt yourself?' When he didn't answer at once, she said, 'That looks a lot like blood in the water and I notice you're moving your left arm a little stiffly.'

You notice too damn much, he told himself, looking into those dark Indian eyes.

'Ran into a nail in the dark last night — down at the fire.'

'Oh, yes. You were helping fight it, weren't you?'

'Me and half the town. Feller dragged me outta bed . . . '

He let the sentence trail off as he watched her face take on a thoughtful look. She straightened a little, turned those dark, all-seeing eyes upon him.

'Strange coincidence, wasn't it?'

He knew what she was talking about

but feigned ignorance. 'What's that?'

'You asking about Bob Dalby after supper — and it was his place where the fire started, according to Barton Gill.'

'That right? Yeah, seems I recollect someone saying it was Dalby's place. But there was so much racket going on, the buildings collapsing and so on. Guess it's lucky we managed to confine the fire to just a couple of places.'

Her eyes narrowed. 'Yes, of course. You all did a fine job. The town could've been destroyed. I wonder whether whoever started the blaze gave that a thought?'

He arched his eyebrows. 'They think it was started deliberately?'

'So I hear,' she said quite sharply. 'I'll repair your undershirt if you'll give it to me to wash first — and your other shirt.'

'Other shirt?'

'The one you were wearing when you hurt yourself. The nail must've torn it, too.'

He nodded. 'Guess so. It's up in my

room. I'll bring it down.'

'All right. What're your plans now?'

Now? He wondered why she had put it that way, as if he had already done something he'd wanted to do and now was ready to move on to the next thing on his agenda.

'I'll be around for a while. Might take a ride out to the range.'

'You're looking for work? You did mention round-up camps last night.'

'Yeah, well it's a while since I've ridden for a spread. But a man has to live. You know of any outfit putting on hands?' She shook her head, then her gaze sharpened as she said,

'You could try Arrowhead. That's the biggest ranch in the county.'

He met and held her gaze, face sober. 'That's the McCord place, isn't it?'

'I believe you know quite well it is.'

He merely nodded. 'Pretty well famous, far beyond just this county. Not keen on working for big spreads, but might try my luck. Thanks for the suggestion.'

39

She smiled crookedly. 'You're a devious man, aren't you, Brett?'

'Me?' All innocence. 'I like to think I'm a straight-from-the-shoulder type.'

'Of course. If I'm mistaken, I apologize.'

'One of us seems to be always apologizing to the other; you notice that?' His amusement somehow annoyed her.

'No, I haven't taken sufficient interest to notice.'

'Well, I could be mistaken. Uh-oh! There we go again . . . I'll go get my other shirt.'

She watched him walk away and realized that she had never seen him without his six-gun riding his right hip, not even at the supper table.

Brett was coming out of his room, the dark bottle-green shirt draped over his left arm, when the sheriff appeared beside him, reached out and took the shirt.

'What we got here, Brett?'

There was another man with him, a deputy, Brett guessed, red-eyed, mighty

40

weary-looking and smelling strongly of woodsmoke. He carried a sawn-off shotgun down at his side, came to about Brett's shoulder; he knew this was the man who had fired at him last night on Blackwood Street.

'Raina's gonna mend my shirt. Tore the sleeve last night on a nail when I was helping fight the fire.'

Barton Gill smiled crookedly. 'No need to remind me, Brett. I was there, too, saw you workin' your butt off. Town owes you thanks.'

'Owes a lot of men.'

'True.' Gill was examining the shirt and poked a finger through the small hole in the left shoulder, making it larger. 'This is more like a hole than a rip from a nail.'

'I fell against it — might've just gone straight in.'

'You better have the doctor look at the wound — rusty nails, you know.'

'It's OK — Raina fixed it.' He told the small lie casually, held out his hand for the shirt.

41

Gill lowered it down to his side out of reach. 'What's that white smear on your boots? Inside, on the edge of the soles, both of 'em.'

Brett felt a sudden gnawing in his belly. What with his haste to get back to his room and then being dragged out to fight the fire, he hadn't had time to scrape the paint flakes from the balcony post off the boots from where he had gripped the wood, sliding down — and climbing back up.

He turned the boots now. The cream paint flakes were obvious. 'Aw, must've been when I stood in some dog's dung. Noticed it when I was on the veranda down below and didn't want to traipse it all over the foyer, so I scraped it off on the bottom of one of them awning posts. Paint's old, must've flaked off when I did it. Leather's porous enough to anchor the flakes there.'

Gill bored his cold eyes into him. 'That's a pretty good answer. You think fast.'

'Not fast enough to know what

42

you're getting at.'

Gill laughed shortly. 'The hell you don't know!' He thrust the shirt back suddenly. 'Want you to stick around town for a spell.'

'Oh? I need to ride out and see if I can find work. I'm a cowhand.'

The deputy snorted. 'Long time since you bull-dogged a maverick an' burned a brand into his hide!'

'What makes you say that?'

'Hell, you're a gunfighter, Brett, we know that! Them callouses on your hands are old. You ain't had a rope burnin' through your palms in years.'

'Now I could take that as you calling me a liar.'

The deputy, Morgan Floyd, stiffened and paled some. He licked his lips. 'Now, wait up! I was just . . . talkin' out loud. Noticed them callouses looked old, that's all. You say they're newer'n I figured, that's OK with me, feller.'

Barton Gill snorted. 'Fast thinkin', Morg! Almost as fast as this ranny with his answers. I want your full name.'

'You've got it.'

Gill made an impatient gesture. ''Brett' ain't good enough! You was seen goin' down that alley leading to Blackwood Street last night, and a few things you've said and done make me think Brett ain't your real name — or only part of it.'

'It's all I go by.'

Gill flushed, started to drop a hand towards his Colt but remembered how fast Brett had got his six-gun out last night. 'You've been here before and you pretend you ain't. I want to know why.'

'If I've been here before it must've been a helluva long time back, 'cause I don't recall it ever happening.'

The sheriff swallowed, barely holding in his anger. 'S'pose I mentioned the name . . . McCord?' When Brett stared back blankly, Gill swore and almost shouted, '*Dan* McCord!'

'Well, I guess he's one of the McCords from Arrowhead but it don't mean spit to me.'

Barton Gill shoved his face closer. 'I

think *you're* Dan McCord!'

Brett frowned. He put his face closer to the lawman's and *sniffed*. Gill jumped back.

'The hell you think you're doin'?'

'Just trying to figure what you been drinking. You don't act drunk but you must be to figure I'm related in any way to the McCords. Hell, man, if I was, I'd be out at that spread right now, with a top hand's job, or even as *segundo*. I'd use whatever clout I had if my name was McCord.'

'I'll stop short of callin' you a liar. But I've spoke to a few folk you've talked to around town and they reckon I could be right.'

'Well, you're wrong. Anyway, has this Dan McCord done something wrong? Broken one of your laws? No? Then what the hell're you bothering me for, Gill?'

Barton Gill started to speak, then clamped his mouth tightly, shook his head. 'Damned if I'll make a fool of myself explainin'! You know damn well what I'm talking about and I'm telling you, *Brett*, or whatever you choose to call yourself — you stay away from the McCords! I hear you've been botherin' Dean or Belle, I'll toss you in my jail so fast your ears'll buzz like a swarm of bees!'

Brett sighed, glanced at the deputy, shook his head slightly. 'Whole blamed town's crazy.'

He walked to the stairs and found Raina standing there near the top. He hadn't realized she was there. He suddenly thrust his shirt towards her.

'I had to come up and make a few beds,' she said, looking at his face carefully. 'I . . . heard the sheriff.'

'Ah, he's got some crazy notion about me being one of the McCords, for Chris — for hell's sakes.'

She surprised him once more when she said in a low voice, 'It could explain quite a few things.'

'Damnit! Not you, too!'

He shouldered roughly past her and stomped down the stairs. Raina glanced

46

up and saw Barton Gill's hard face looking over the banister.

'I think he's come back to square things,' the sheriff said quietly.

'It's hard to believe. It must be — what — fifteen years? I was very young when we came here.'

'Closer to seventeen or eighteen. Just before you arrived with your ma and she opened the roomin' house.'

'Yes, that's right. We heard a little about it, but wouldn't Brett be too old?'

'Danny was around sixteen when he left.'

'Brett looks older than mid-thirties.'

'If he's the *hombre* I'm thinkin' of, he's led a mighty rough life, the kind that ages a man. Livin' on a knife-edge, you know? Gunfights, bounty huntin'. Big strain on any man and can put grey in your hair mighty fast.'

'Well, I really don't know much about it, but . . . ' She paused and her white teeth tugged briefly at her full lower lip. She frowned a little, trying to make her mind up, then said, 'He did

47

ask if Bob Dalby was still in town.'

The sheriff's mouth pulled into a tight line, as he straightened. '*Did* he now! Well, well, well! I wonder how he knew that name if he ain't Dan McCord?'

'What does Dalby have to do with it?'

'Aw, Bob dabbles in things. A little smoky, you know what I mean? but mostly manages to stay clear of steppin' outside the law.'

'Mostly?'

Gill nodded. 'Been a coupla times — nothin' too serious, but he come close to seein' the inside of my jail. Was said once he got himself outta trouble with Big Al McCord by putting the blame on young Danny. Some steers was sold on a forged ownership paper. Caused one helluva ruckus among the McCords, and Dan had a fallin'-out with Al. They say Al took a whip to him and the kid went haywire, somehow took it offa Al, then belted him over the head with a fence post. Cracked his skull, almost killed him. But the kid lit

48

out and ain't never been back.' He twisted his mouth under the moustache, adding, 'Far as we know.'

'And you think that now this man Brett is really Dan McCord, and has come back, eighteen years on, to even the scores he thinks he has to settle?'

'Seems possible to me. I mean he knows his way around town and this is a pretty *big* town for these parts. Knew Bob Dalby's place was on Blackwood Street, knew that Rowley had been Dowd's original pardner in the livery — Things a man who'd lived here would know about . . . '

'I see. But does he look like Dan McCord?'

Gill shrugged. 'Baby-faced kid of sixteen ain't gonna look anywheres near the same in his thirties. Specially if them years've been hard and rough.'

'Ye-es. I suppose it would be difficult to see an easy resemblance. I'd never heard the full story before.' Raina seemed nervous, as if she was sorry she had precipitated this.

'Well, I figure we're all gonna hear about it pretty soon, and we'll see what happens now Danny boy's all growed up and primed for bear.'

'We might see it,' Morg Floyd opined, 'if the gunsmoke ain't too damn thick.'

★　★　★

Brett smoothed the saddle blanket on the roan's back and the horse snorted slightly, flicked its pale tail and turned its head to look at him with big brown eyes.

'Yeah, ol' pard, we're taking us a little ride. Can't have you growing fat on oats and no exercise.'

He threw the saddle across, settled it in to a comfortable position and reached under for the cinch strap.

While he was occupied doing this, Phil Rowley, hay fork in hand, walked casually to the big open doorway, glanced towards the saloon across the street and lifted the fork on to his shoulder, twisted it twice. He paused, then turned and walked back down the aisle, began pitching hay from the stockpile into the nearest stall.

Brett had just taken the bridle from the wall peg when he was aware of the light changing in the stall. He glanced over his shoulder and saw two men standing in the entrance, hazy silhouettes.

One was big and beefy, and wore two guns, butt foremost. The other was tall, too, a good size, but not as big as the first. Shifting light touched a narrow face which gleamed with unguent rubbed over several scorched places. He gave the impression that the eyebrows had been singed almost completely away.

Brett turned slowly and deliberately. 'Starting to show a belly, Bob?'

'I'll show you more than my belly, you son of a bitch! You said you'd be back and I didn't believe you. Took your damn time! Nigh on eighteen years — and first thing you do is ruin me!'

51

'Heard a fire wiped you out last night. Bad luck.'

'Sure is — for some,' allowed the big man, his voice deep, rumbling around a barrel chest.

Bob Dalby grinned tightly, gestured towards his big companion. 'This is Nick Holt. Works for me. Kind of a watchdog, takes care of . . . awkward chores, you know?'

''Bout time he started earning his money, ain't it?' Both men frowned at Brett's words; he had edged around so he could see them better in the sunlight now. 'I mean, he didn't do much of a job last night, did he? Let someone burn you out.'

Holt started forward and Bob Dalby lifted a hand, then changed his mind, dropped it to his side and nodded to the big man.

'He's right, Nick. Start earning your money!'

Holt was impatient to get at Brett and hadn't noticed the bridle because of the corner shadow in the stall. The

52

big man took a long step forward, then he gave a startled yell as the bridle *swished*! and sweat-hardened leather-and-metal joining-rings slammed him in the face. His head jerked and he stumbled back, bringing a curse from Dalby, who was knocked off balance.

Brett surged forward, slashing right and left with the bridle, leaving Holt and forcing Dalby out into the aisle away from the frightened roan, which was beginning to stomp and whicker.

Holt clawed at his face; trickles of blood were crawling between his big fingers. Bob Dalby had regained his balance, a welt showing on one cheek, a cut on the other. His eyes blazed as he ducked under Brett's next swing but felt as if his head was almost torn from his shoulders by a lifting knee that smashed into his forehead.

He shot back, arms spread and flailing as he crashed into the wall opposite. His scrabbling boots slid in the damp straw and the urine that trickled from the occupied stalls. He sat down with a thump, gasping.

Brett swung up the bridle again but Holt lunged forward, grabbed it and pulled Brett off balance. Holt didn't have a good enough grip on the bridle to use it with any force, and Brett felt it crack across his shoulders. He straightened as Holt threw the bridle aside and, baring his teeth through a mask of blood, stepped forward, trying to stomp on Brett's instep even as he swung a punch.

His boot missed but the fist skidded along Brett's jaw, sending him reeling. He hit the aisle end of the stall partition, his head ringing. Holt charged, both big fists working and hammering. Brett was jolted by the blows, heavy, punishing, bending his ribs, driving the breath from him.

Nick Holt was an experienced fighter: hammer a man's body, get him short of breath and gasping in pain, then quickly shift the attack to the face and head. When a man's worried about his midriff, his arms are heading that way to protect from further injury — or have already arrived, leaving his upper body and head unprotected.

This is what happened, and although Brett reacted mighty fast and got his hands up again, three straight rights and a left smashed him back against the wall. Horses were plunging and snorting and whinnying, one at least kicking at the plank stall-dividers. Quite a racket.

But all Brett could hear were the noises filling his head from the punishing blows. He felt his left leg begin to buckle, made an effort to straighten it, but his boot slipped. He went down to one knee. It happened fast, caught Holt unawares. He had been concentrating on battering Brett's face and now his fists blurred forward before he could stop. They passed over Brett's head as he dropped and, with instinct born of a hundred past brawls, some of them literally a fight for life, he rammed a fist upwards, feeling his knuckles crush into Holt's crotch.

The big man gave a strangled cry and started to sag, hands automatically reaching for the pain zone. Brett shoulder-rolled out from under, twisted in time to sweep his legs around and bring down the stumbling Bob Dalby. The stock agent thudded to the aisle beside him; Brett twisted fingers in the man's brown hair and rapped his head twice on the ground. Dalby sagged but Brett was no longer interested in him.

He straightened as Holt, leaning a sagging shoulder against an awning post, looked up with pain-contorted face. He must have registered that Brett was coming after him and he grunted loudly, turned it into a roar of effort as he raged upright.

Brett weaved aside, stepped in and hammered the man's side ribs, and, as he half-turned, belted two punishing blows into Holt's kidneys. It gave Holt pause — *painful* pause — and his legs buckled. Brett slugged him on the jaw, used his knees to ram the man into the wall, then clubbed him on the back of his neck. Holt sprawled on his face in the muck and slush of the stables' aisle, came up spitting, blood-streaked face contorted with rage.

He ran four steps up the aisle then abruptly turned, both hands whipping across his body to his six-guns.

Brett hadn't been expecting it but reacted faster than a man can blink, taking a side leap to the left, bringing up his Colt with his right hand.

All three guns blazed simultaneously, filling the livery with their thunder and roiling smoke.

This was swiftly followed by a single shot — from Brett's Colt. Nick Holt, already falling, mouth sagging open and spilling blood, was wrenched violently to the right, bounced off the nearest awning post and hit the floor rolling. But it was only a roll caused by the strike of the bullet, and he flopped back on his face, fancy snakeskin half-boots rapping the floor in a brief tattoo.

★ ★ ★

57

When Sheriff Barton Gill came running, gripping a short-barrelled Ithaca shotgun, he skidded to a halt and looked at the scene before him.

By now almost a dozen townsfolk who had been on the street and heard the gunfire had crowded inside and were pushing into the aisle, jostling to see who was shot.

At first it was a little hard to tell. Bob Dalby was sitting with his back to a stall partition, shirt blood-spattered, his face bruised and swollen, eyes shut. Across from him, Brett was slumped with his back against an awning post, blood and stable muck all over his clothes, a still smoking six-gun in his limp right hand resting on the ground beside him.

But there could be no mistake about Nick Holt. Blood ran from under his twisted body in snaking rivers. What could be seen of his face was far from pretty, one cheek torn away, a mess of brutalized flesh and splintered bone.

'Hell almighty!' Gill breathed, setting his gaze on Brett and lifting the shotgun barrels just enough to cover him. Then he smiled slowly, thumbed back both hammers. 'Why, I do b'lieve I've got the best reason in the world to lock you up now, Brett! My lucky day!'

'I seen it all, Bart.'

All eyes turned to sweating Phil Rowley as he pushed roughly through the crowd, leaning on the long-handled hay fork. He gestured to Brett who had swivelled his half-open eyes towards him. 'He started the fight, beat Nick somethin' awful about the head with a bridle. Then when things got tough an' Bob joined in to help Nick, Brett went for his gun! Nick turned to run, as I thought, but runnin' ain't in Nick's line. He spun back, reachin' for his own guns, and if he hadn't turned this Brett woulda shot him in the back! He's a damn killer, Bart!'

'An' you,' gasped Brett, 'you're a — goddamned — lyin' son of a bitch!'

He struggled to bring his Colt up but Barton Gill kicked the weapon from his hand, stood above him, the shotgun

59

barrels inches from Brett's chest.

'We'll continue this down at the jailhouse, and, I was you, I wouldn't bother orderin' lunch at the Redbird.' Grinning now, the sheriff added, 'Nor supper, nor anythin' else. Raina can rent your room out any time she likes, 'cause you ain't gonna have any more use for it.'

4

Family?

Brett was dozing on the hard, narrow bunk when the rattling of the cell door disturbed him.

He started to sit up, groaned involuntarily. There was a neat bandage around his head and a plaster pulled taut against the skin on his left tricep where it covered the small buckshot wound. Other bandages were wrapped tightly around his lower ribs. The rest of him *ached* as if he'd been run over by stampeding cattle. He smiled ruefully: actually, he had been, a long time ago.

The town doctor had done an efficient job and Brett figured he would be feeling a lot worse if the sawbones hadn't tended him. Still, the fussy old devil had caused him some trouble: he had spotted the inflamed buckshot wound and washed it with antiseptic, probed deep and pulled out a jagged piece of lead that Brett had missed.

Barton Gill had been standing by in the cell, with his shotgun, taking no chances with Brett, and the medic had said, 'I've seen enough gunshot wounds to say this is a piece off a shotgun pellet. Ricocheted, I would think, broke up before entering the flesh.'

The sheriff had leered at the exhausted Brett. 'Now that might just put you at the scene of Bob Dalby's fire last night, Brett, old hoss, before you joined the bucket brigade, that is. Deputy Foyle got a shot at someone he seen slinkin' around there an' was sure he hit him. Doc, you sure that ain't just a wound from fallin' against a rusty nail?'

'Most definitely not.'

That had pleased the lawman and even through his pain and fatigue, Brett knew he was in a deal of trouble.

He didn't know how long ago that was, because he had been dozing on

62

and off, catnapping. Now, head throbbing, he squinted against sunlight streaming in through the high barred window and saw the sheriff at the door with two people. One was a woman, wearing a split riding-skirt, slapping a fancy quirt with Indian beading on the handle against her left leg. He had an impression of fair hair showing under the narrow-brimmed hat, couldn't see her face too well because of the shadows. She was maybe in her mid-to-late twenties.

The man, around forty, was medium tall, solidly built, wore leather chaps over faded, work-worn denim trousers, and a sweat-stained grey shirt with a rip on one shoulder. He packed a six-gun, carelessly pushed around towards his back. What Brett could see of his face was deeply tanned, clean-shaven, with a thrusting jaw, and bleak-looking pale grey eyes, above a bent nose. *Like Big Al McCord's* . . .

'Folks to see you,' Barton announced suddenly. 'Recognize 'em?'

63

Brett struggled up and swung his legs slowly over the side of the bunk. He made no attempt to approach the cell door.

'I'll take a guess. The lady's Belle McCord and the man's her brother, Dean.' *That ought to stir them up!*

Barton's mouth twisted sardonically. 'Good guess!' He turned to the McCords. 'Reckon this is your kid brother, Danny, folks?'

'Adopted brother,' Dean corrected him, coming right up to the bars and staring hard. 'I — dunno. Could be. What you say, sis?'

The girl stepped up beside him. Clear, cool, green eyes gave Brett a good working-over.

'He could be. But his hair's darker, his build is different and — well, I plain don't know, but I expect a man in his thirties would look different from when he was only a gangling boy of fifteen.' She had a pleasant enough voice and right now it sounded puzzled, but those eyes were hostile. 'Are you claiming to

64

be Danny McCord?' she asked.

'Sheriff reckons I am. I go by the name of Brett.'

He watched her closely, saw the immediate frown and tension in her. She flicked her eyes to her brother.

'Mother's maiden name!'

'If you are Danny, why change your name?' Dean snapped.

'McCord was never my name.'

'It was the one Pa gave you! And damn lucky you were! You should've felt privileged to wear the McCord name!'

'Why choose Ma's maiden name?' Belle persisted.

'Maybe because she was the only one treated an orphaned kid decent. Lot better than the rest of you. But after she died, you had a free hand and made the most of it.'

'You damned ungrateful son of a bitch! Pa dragged you out of a smashed-up wagon, with your family lyin' dead and mutilated by Indians! He gave you a *home* as well as a name! He

65

reared you! And how did you show your gratitude?' Dean's mouth curled and his knuckles whitened where his hands gripped the bars. 'By selling off the herd Pa trusted you with to take to the sale-yards! Stole the money, and then tried to throw the blame on to Bob Dalby, an innocent man you duped!'

'A fifteen-year-old kid did all that?' Brett said, standing a little shakily now and shuffling towards the bars. 'Fooled a stock agent, meat buyer, got cash instead of a bank draft? Don't reckon I was ever that smart.'

Dean stepped back when he saw the battered face, and those tombstone eyes drilling into him.

'You two were ready to believe whatever they said. You *wanted* 'Danny Boy' out of Arrowhead.'

'Why don't you stop speaking about yourself in the third person?' snapped Belle.

Brett smiled thinly. 'Who said I'm speaking about myself?'

'What?' She looked perplexed, flicked

her gaze to Dean and the frowning sheriff. 'You won't even admit that you are Danny, grown up?'

'I use the name Brett. Already told you.'

'This is getting us nowhere,' Belle said curtly. 'He's just as — cantankerous — as he was as a kid — worse, if I recollect. The thing is, he's back to cause trouble, and already has, for Bob Dalby — '

'Could've burned the whole blamed town,' growled Gill, 'if that fire'd gotten outta control. As it is, Donahue's lost his horse-breeding records just because his office was next to Bob's. And Will Bayliss, t'other side, won't be able to use his place again without a major rebuild.'

'Never mind that,' snapped Dean, face taut and pale now as he stared at Brett. 'Why did you come back?'

'Back? This is my first visit here.'

Barton Gill snorted. 'Sure it is! You know the streets and folks' business like you been livin' here for twenty years!

You're up to no good, mister, and I mean to see that whatever you were plannin' ends right here in this cell!'

He looked at the McCords for approval but their faces showed nothing, except maybe some trepidation.

'Town feels mighty riled about that fire. How easy it coulda run wild and wiped out the whole kit-and-caboodle.' Gill looked directly at Dean. 'I take him to court and charge him with arson, an' mebbe a few other things, like the killin' of Nick Holt, and this feller's gonna spend the rest of his life on the rockpile. If the judge don't stretch his neck.' He smirked as Brett stiffened. 'That woke you up proper, didn't it?'

'Holt went for his guns first.'

'Not according to Rowley — and Bob Dalby.'

'Two to one against. Well, guess I lose that one.'

'You lose, period!'

Brett glanced at the McCords. 'Must've been worth your while to ride twelve miles just to hear that, huh?'

'Yes!' said the girl quickly. 'I'd be happy to see you punished!'

'If you've never been here before,' Dean said slowly, 'how come you know Arrowhead is twelve miles outta town?'

'Lucky guess.'

The girl was angry, slapping her leg harder and faster with the quirt now; if it hurt, she didn't seem to notice. 'You almost killed our father! After all he'd done for you! He — he was never the same after you hit him with that fence post. Slow-moving, slow-thinking, indecisive . . . '

Brett's shirt had been hanging loose and he pulled it down over his shoulders now, turning, letting them see his scarred back, or as much as showed above the bandages.

'You deserved a whipping!' she snapped, a sob at the edge of her voice.

'Deserved a helluva lot more — and now he's gonna get it,' Dean added. 'Sheriff, you want to charge him, go ahead, but charge him as 'Brett'. We'd rather not have the McCord name blackened by the likes of him!'

The girl nodded vigorously. 'Yes! I agree!'

'Then rest easy, folks. I've always had plenty of respect for Big Al and Judge Ethan was one of Al's close friends. It'll be pure pleasure to charge this sonuver with everythin' I can think of and get him put away for good.' He leaned towards the bars. 'Or, if I could prove he was the one backshot your father . . . Be no skulkin' then, mister!'

'You haven't lynched me yet, Gill.'

'Now *there*'s an idea! *Lynchin'!* Save the town the expense of a trial! Good thinkin', Brett, good thinkin'.'

What Brett noticed most was that neither Dean nor Belle McCord made any protest.

★   ★   ★

When the street door opened and slowly swung back against the wall, Barton Gill looked up irritably from the pile of ragged wanted dodgers he had

70

been examining. He pulled his half-moon spectacles down his nose as Raina Redbird eased awkwardly into the law office, carrying a cloth-covered tray.

'What the hell're you doin' here?'

'I always bring food for your prisoners, Sheriff, you surely know that.'

He grunted. 'Hadn't even thought about it. You might wait till you're asked next time. I gotta find money from my funds to pay for this kinda thing.' He gestured towards the tray.

She lifted a corner of the cloth and he saw several dishes. 'Some soup — bacon and fried potatoes — a slice of cold apple pie — and coffee. Totals up to about thirty-five cents. Can the law office afford that?'

He scowled, jerked his head towards the door that led to the cell block. 'Don't stay gabbin' to him. Just slide it through the slot and leave.' As she started towards the door he suddenly stood and came around his desk,

71

whipping the covering cloth off entirely. He picked up the cutlery, kept the knife and fork, left the spoon. 'Won't be the first time Brett's ate with his fingers.'

'Oh? You're still calling him 'Brett'? I thought you'd decided he was Danny McCord.' Her voice hardened. 'At least, that's what the men gathering outside the saloon and sprawling all over my porch are saying.'

Gill looked innocent, didn't speak.

'They're drinking a lot and muttering, too. It sounds like lynch talk, to me. Sheriff, I think you should go down there and break up what could turn into a mob.'

'You do, huh? Well, you stick to runnin' your roomin' house, and I'll look after the law. Now get a move on. I want my own supper.'

As she went through the door to the cell block, tray skilfully balanced on one hand, she said, 'My kitchen's closed for the night.'

His mouth tightened. He glared at her just before the door closed behind

72

her. His stomach growled at the savoury smells left hanging in the stuffy air of the office.

'Goddamn squaw!'

Brett moved slowly off the bunk, watching the Indian girl as she pushed the food tray through the slot cut in the barred door.

'I'm obliged, Raina.'

'Barton Gill allows me to provide meals for his prisoners. Of course, he expects some kind of ... consideration.' Brett looked up sharply as he straightened with the tray. She smiled, adding, 'He eats cheaply at my dining room. In fact, most times for free.'

'So, he's not such a stickler for the law as he makes out when it comes to himself, eh?'

'Go ahead and eat. I'll collect the tray later.' She turned away, then paused, sober now. 'I think you should know, there's some harsh talk about town. Many people are hostile towards you because of the danger you placed us all in by lighting that fire.'

73

He looked up from spooning soup to his sore mouth. 'I'm s'posed to've lit it?'

'It was a . . . reckless thing to do,' she admonished, though she couldn't see that her words or disapproval had any effect on him. 'Very dangerous!'

'Saw the firehouse and the old pump wagon standing outside it when I first arrived. I'm not saying I did or didn't light that fire, but if I had, seeing that would've made me think the town wasn't in much danger.'

He gave her a challenging look and she seemed briefly embarrassed.

'But you took a terrible chance! All because of what Bob Dalby supposedly did to you almost twenty years earlier.'

His eyes locked with hers. 'Because of what he *did*.'

She thought she knew what he was trying to tell her and it only added to her confusion. 'I . . . don't quite understand you. From what I gather, Al McCord raised you and you — turned on him. Now, if I see things correctly, you're here to destroy his family!'

74

He looked at her, jaws working on the food, for a long minute. He knew his next words could even hang him, but he felt he could be a little more open with this woman.

'Too bad he died before I got here.'

She stiffened. 'My God! You — you would've *killed* Big Al McCord?'

He merely picked up a strip of bacon and chewed a piece off, his mouth moving in such a way that she knew it was very hot. She hoped it burned his tongue!

'I don't know who you really are, but . . . there could be a lynching! If there is, you've brought it on yourself.'

'That's a comfort to know.'

She felt her cheeks burning. She almost paused to apologize, but then went on down the passage and closed the cell block door behind her.

Brett continued eating, enjoying the well-cooked meal.

'*And the condemned man ate a hearty last meal!*' he murmured without humour.

75

★   ★   ★

It was full dark when Raina opened the front door of her rooming house and stepped out on to the porch.

It was crowded with men now, some standing, some sitting on the edge. Several bottles were being passed around and there were a couple of whistles when she appeared.

'Come sit here, sweetheart. I'll make room for you.'

'Ah, she'll get splinters. Sit on my knee instead.'

'She gets splinters, I'll take 'em out for her!'

That got a laugh and it was shouted on across the alley to where a larger group of raucous men were gathering.

'Can't you men go someplace else for your mischief?' she snapped, forcing her way down the short steps to the boardwalk. 'This is a rooming house, not a meeting-place.'

'I'll go — if you'll come with me, honey!'

Cramped by the men around her, Raina smiled and reached into her apron pocket. Suddenly there was a cleared space around her.

'She's got a knife!' someone yelled.

Raina removed a short, well-honed and well-used blade from a beaded sheath. It was Indian-made, and for one obvious purpose. She raised it, let the back of the blade touch her hairline to give them the idea as she smiled coldly.

'Be careful with your offers of fraternization, gentlemen. I haven't used my knife for quite some time, but ... I rather like the idea of decorating some new curtains I'm making for my dining room with a head or two of white man's hair. One red, one black, I think, or maybe flaxen — yes, perhaps that.' She looked pointedly at some of the men close by. Lights from the saloon glinted on the honed steel. 'Then, of course, if necessary, this blade can be used a little ... lower down.' She dropped her gaze slowly and there was no mistaking where she was looking.

The space around her grew rapidly larger.

'Why don't you go home, the lot of you! You all talk loudly but that's all it is — drunken talk. Just look at you! Twenty or more men, so-called, trying to get up enough courage to attack one wounded man alone in a cell! Oh, my! What a lot of heroes you are! If I was the wife of any one of you — God forbid! — I'd twist your ear and drag you off home.'

There was a silence and then someone said, rather lamely, 'You can twist my ear an' drag me off, any time, sweetmeat!'

But it fell like a lead balloon. None of them liked being bettered by a woman on Main Street — sure not an Indian woman.

'Ah, go to hell, you Injun bitch!' someone called.

Raina smiled faintly as she sheathed the knife, hurried across the street and down to the law office.

Deputy Foyle was dozing behind the desk, but jumped up, startled, when she entered. She could smell whiskey.

'What you want?'

'I've come to collect the prisoner's supper tray.'

'Aw, yeah. Bart said you might be in. Get your tray an' go on home.'

'Why're you hurrying me, Deputy?'

'I'll hurry you if I want! This is the law office an' your business oughtn't take more'n a few minutes. Now get it done.'

'Where's the sheriff?'

'None of your business. You gonna move?'

'Certainly,' she said stiffly and went into the cell block. The passage was dimly lit by only one oil lamp.

There was just enough light for her to see Brett getting stiffly off his bunk and coming to the door. He nudged the tray out through the slot.

'You're a damn fine cook, Raina.'

'Here's some dessert,' she said in a

79

quiet voice. He frowned.

'But I already had the slice of . . . ' He stiffened when he felt the cold metal of a small gun against his hand. His fingers closed over it instinctively. Looking down, he saw that it was a twin-barrelled derringer: by its weight he reckoned it was the larger version in .41 calibre. Before he could speak, she showed him the sheathed knife; he took it swiftly, pushed it into his belt.

'I'm obliged, but you're making a lot of trouble for yourself.'

'Men are gathering on the street. They're in an ugly mood and there's lynch talk. Bob Dalby is haranguing a drunken mob in the saloon bar and it'll come as no surprise when I tell you Barton Gill's nowhere to be seen. D'you know the Whetstones?'

He hesitated briefly, then nodded. 'Reckon I can find my way around well enough. I've heard it's a good place to hide.'

She frowned at his words. 'You don't sound very . . . confident. Almost as if you've never been there before — '

'The hell you doin' in there?' Foyle yelled suddenly. 'I gotta come after you, I'll kick your butt — '

'Coming!' she called. She threw Brett a quick smile and, rattling the dishes as she hurried away, said loudly and irritably: 'Why don't you put an extra lamp in the passage?'

Angrily, she appeared before Foyle at the front office door, juggling the tray. 'I tripped back there and it's a wonder my dishes didn't break. If they had, I'd want full compensation. My grandmother made those dishes out of clay from the river beside the camp where I was born and they mean a lot to me . . . '

'Yeah, yeah. Mean spit to me. Now get goin'. This ain't no place for you.'

'I think I agree with you, Deputy.'

He slammed the street door after her, made sure the lock hadn't engaged and went back behind the desk. His stomach was clenched, his mouth dry. He glanced at the big, loud-ticking

81

railroad clock on the wall above the gun rack . . .

Another half-hour before they came. Time enough to toss down another couple of snorts from the whiskey bottle he had stashed behind the gun rack. And, man, did he need them!

5

Necktie Party

'Deputy! Deputy! Get in here, man! I-I think that damn squaw's — poisoned — me!'

Brett made loud retching sounds, got down on one knee beside the bunk, head hanging, face shielded by his left arm. When he heard the passage door open he retched again, adding a hacking cough and spitting.

'Aw, Judas! What'd she put — in that — slop she called — soup . . . ' He made appropriate sounds again as Foyle, reeking of booze, reached the door.

The deputy looked puzzled, not quite alert after all the whiskey he had poured down his throat.

'Wha-what the hell're you playin' at?'

Brett moaned realistically. 'Thought

it was — queer — the way she said — 'Enjoy your — soup, Paleface — I made it specially for you!' Hell, it tasted fine an . . . '

Starting to swing away from the bars, Foyle growled, 'Ah, you'll be all right. I got no time for this — '

'How about for this?'

Brett came swiftly to his feet and held the cocked derringer on the startled deputy.

'Huh? Wha — ? Where you get that?'

'All you need worry about is I've got it, Foyle. Open the door or I'll take your kneecap off.'

Foyle, brain hazy, frowned. 'L'il thing like that?'

'Forty-one calibre. I cut a cross in the nose of the bullets. They'll spread like a mushroom when they hit, tear half your leg off.'

Foyle felt sick; one ear was listening for the mob that should be here mighty soon — but maybe not soon enough. Luckily, Brett's imitation of a retching man had been good enough for the

84

deputy instinctively to grab the cell keys when he started into the jail area.

He fumbled badly, kept looking at the derringer only inches from his leg, the barrel poking between the bars for a clear shot. But the lock tumblers clanked and Foyle, with a sudden burst of courage, dragged the door open quickly and tried to kick Brett.

The prisoner turned aside but the boot skidded across his thigh. He staggered and Foyle groped for his six-gun. Brett, holding the little gun in his palm, smashed it into the deputy's face. The weapon was surprisingly heavy for a small gun, but loaded, so it had the extra weight of the cartridges behind it when it slammed between Foyle's reddened eyes. He grunted and fell to his knees. Brett clubbed him across the back of the neck with a hammer blow of his fist, dragged his unconscious body into the cell and rolled it under the bunk. He wrenched the Colt from the man's holster, slammed and locked the cell door, and hurried down to the front office. He used the blade of Raina's knife to prise the padlock from the gun cupboard door, the screws pulling easily enough out of the old wood. His own six-gun rig was lying on the bottom shelf; he buckled it about his waist quickly.

He froze as he settled the rig comfortably. A sound like the roar of a distant cataract was drawing closer. He recognized it — having once before been the target of a drunken lynch party. The mob were coming for him.

He snatched his rifle from the gun rack and grabbed a box of cartridges. Then he locked the street door and dropped the bar into place.

The mob were hammering on the door as he left by the rear. He groped his way across the dark yard, hesitated at the stables, but heard glass breaking and ran for the sagging rear fence.

There was a creek which, he knew, ran down behind the tannery that stood behind the livery stables. He smelled the stinking tanning pools with their soaking hides and skirted them. He heard yells and a wild shot in the night, but they were well behind him now. The bulk of the livery loomed over the corrals and he figured that if he was this close to his own horse then he might as well take the extra risk and try to get to it.

Phil Rowley was waiting in the shadows with his two-pronged hay fork. He lunged at Brett as the man turned into the stall where his roan stood.

'Figured you'd try for your bronc!'

Brett jumped aside as the fork drove at him. Rowley's considerable weight was behind it and the tines drove into the partition, jammed in the wood.

Before the livery man could pull the fork free the rifle butt slammed across Rowley's head. The fat man gave a kind of sigh and sagged to his knees. Another blow from the rifle stretched him out. Brett heaved him into the aisle, dropped the gun while he grabbed his saddle from the top of the partition and threw it across the roan's back.

87

'Have to skip the banket this time, boy,' he said as the horse tried to nuzzle him. 'We've got to *move*!'

There was quite a racket on Main now as he led the roan to the rear of the big building and out into the night. Men were yelling, some were cursing.

'Get to the livery!' He recognized Bob Dalby's agitated voice, and boots drummed rapidly, coming fast towards the front entrance. Time he wasn't here!

He swung aboard, rifle in his left hand, jammed the rein ends between his teeth and kicked in his heels.

The roan took off, down past the corrals, its passage causing some of the milling animals there to whinny — which might bring the lynch mob to investigate.

It did, and there were wild yells mixed with several gunshots. Just for the hell of it, he twisted in the saddle and raked the livery entrance with three rapid shots, sending splinters flying. He had the impression of men scattering as he swung away towards the creek. The

88

roan splashed across and up the far bank. Brett recalled the lie of the land now, eased around the tanning pools and kept the tannery building between himself and where he figured the mob to be as he spurred away into the night.

Distantly, the Whetstones loomed against the stars, beckoning, a place of thick timber and deep canyons: one of them was called 'Gunbutt'. He hoped he could find it!

As a volley of gunfire rattled behind him he leaned forward over the roan's arching neck. 'Make some mileage, boy!' he whispered into one laid-back ear.

It was time to run: the time to stand and fight would come soon enough. Probably too damn soon!

* * *

Raina didn't know where the sheriff had come from but he was in a mighty bad mood when Foyle, gripping her upper arm more tightly than he needed,

89

dragged her into the law office. He thrust her towards a chair in front of the desk. Barton Gill was at the gun rack, thumbing short red cardboard cylinders into a shotgun, the brass bases with their copper percussion caps glinting briefly in the lamplight.

Foyle, hair dripping from where he had dunked it hurriedly in the horse trough to try and sober up before Gill arrived, stood stiffly beside the girl.

'She's known to pack a derringer, Bart! An' that one Brett had was fancy, pearl grips, engravin' on the sides.'

Gill ignored him, snapped the shotgun closed and placed it on the desk. The barrels were pointing in Raina's general direction, either by accident or design.

She drew down a deep, anxious breath, sat straighter in the chair. 'D'you mind pointing that gun elsewhere, Sheriff?'

'It's OK as it is,' Gill growled, leaning forward, resting one hand on the gun. 'Why'd you help Brett escape?'

'Who said I did?' She reared back, gasping, as his open hand slapped her across the face, the white imprint of his fingers showing against the golden skin. There were tears of pain in her dark eyes as she rubbed the place.

'I'm in no mood for smart talk from a damn squaw who ought to be washin' dishes in some kitchen, instead of runnin' the place.'

She narrowed her eyes; most folk were used to her owning the rooming house, left to her by her white mother, by now. It was a long time since anyone had openly shown their racial hostility and it surprised her some — but, seeing as it was Barton Gill, not too much. He was an envious man.

'You collected his meal tray and when you left he pulled a derringer on this idiot.' Gill gestured to Deputy Foyle whose ears coloured and his lips tightened but he said nothing. 'You gave Brett the gun all right.'

'It sounds like it could be my derringer,' she admitted slowly, her

91

burning gaze making the angry sheriff feel a mite uneasy. 'I carry it when I go out at night.' She gave him a crooked smile. 'Even your street patrols can't keep a squaw woman entirely safe, Barton.'

He made a threatening gesture with the back of his hand and she winced, instinctively jerking away. He smiled.

'This is a no-holds-barred situation, Raina.'

'I-I realize it's serious, Sheriff, but if you'll give me a moment . . . As I said, I do carry a derringer in my pocket if I'm out on the streets at night for any reason. I . . . recall now that Brett fumbled the tray against the bars and I did feel his hand briefly on my . . . front. It's possible he took the gun then, could've easily palmed it. Then Foyle started yelling at me and there were drunks on the street. I was quite . . . rattled. I only wanted to get back to my place, and I . . . just never missed it.' Gill stared hard at her, his face unreadable. 'It could've happened that way, Sheriff,' she said trying to keep the desperation out of her voice. 'I-I have no interest in seeing Brett go free, after the way he endangered the entire town. My rooming house is only one street away from where he set that fire, after all.'

Gill grunted, still glaring. 'I ought to lock you up, just to be sure, but I'll need a lot of food for the posse, so you go pack some grubsacks — and don't send no bill to the county afterwards, you savvy?'

'I understand. You're being high-handed, Sheriff, and exceeding your authority — '

'Foyle!' interrupted Gill angrily. 'Take her through and lock her up! I got no time for this.'

'Wait!' Raina said quickly, her heart hammering against her ribs. 'I-I'll prepare some food for your men. How many will there be?'

'Half the goddamn town's after him already,' Foyle said, but then fell silent at a glare from Gill.

93

'I'll take six good men with me. *Good* men, which lets you out, Foyle. You go with Raina and see she does her chore properly. An' don't think this is the end of it, Miss Lakota! You'll be here when I get back — with Brett — and we'll sort things out then.' He turned to the deputy again. 'I'm leavin' her in your charge, so don't foul up!'

Foyle drew himself up. 'Don't worry none, Bart. She'll be here waitin' for you.'

'If she ain't, you better not be.' Foyle jerked his head towards the door, beyond which they could still hear all the shouting of the half-drunk men assembling, hoping to be chosen for the posse; the county paid seventy-five cents a day for a manhunt like this one and, with a little luck, it could escalate.

★ ★ ★

Raina was worried after her clash with Barton Gill.

She knew he was a hard man, given

to capricious moods, and sometimes excessive violence when making arrests. She was still trembling; she had come so close to being locked up, which was the last thing she wanted.

She was committed now to Brett, although she still wasn't sure who he was. Danny McCord or just — Brett, whoever that might be. There was something very strange about him: he knew so much about this town and its people. He *had* to have grown up here, at least until he was fifteen or sixteen years old. And yet — why didn't he either admit he was Danny McCord or come straight out and say he wasn't?

She paused: he *had* done that. Several times. And then something would happen that made people believe he must be Dan McCord. How else could he possibly know all about the McCords' doings? How could he know the streets so well, the locations of buildings, people's names, their backgrounds?

She had been only a child when he

95

was supposed to have quit the McCords after fracturing Big Al McCord's skull. A frightened fifteen-year-old, afraid he had killed the man who had raised him.

And that was strange: Brett did not seem the kind of man who would be so ungrateful. Just an . . . instinct, nothing she could say she definitely *knew*; perhaps it was her Lakota blood, but she felt he was a decent man. An unforgiving one, perhaps, but basically decent.

'Come on! Don't be all damn day or Bart'll come ragin' in here and I'll be the one who feels the back of his hand this time!'

Foyle was mighty nervous, guilty because he had been caught with whiskey on his breath, half-drunk, when the lynch party was supposed to take place. He was more afraid of Gill than she was.

Raina had set out seven flour sacks and was emptying her cupboards to fill them with the supplies the men would need on wilderness trails. She gave the bare amount necessary of bacon and jerky, flour, cooking grease, cracked corn, coffee and sugar; she put in a couple of cans of peaches, some salt and spices — she did not stint on the chili powder, just placed it in a cardboard container simply labelled 'Spice'.

The more uncomfortable she could make it for the posse, the worse the job they would make of the pursuit. Foyle was too nervous to notice much; she plied him with coffee, and, at the third cup, said, quietly, persuasively,

'You seem to have the shakes, Deputy. I do have a little brandy if you'd like a . . . hand-steadier in your coffee?'

She could see right away he was tempted. But he was afraid of Barton Gill, too, and said, gruffly, 'I don't need nothin'. But mebbe after the posse leaves town, eh?'

She smiled at his conspiratorial wink; she would see that he had quite a good slug and not all of it would be brandy. Her mother, long used to handling aggressive and amorous drunks, had always kept a supply of something she called *sleepytime* on hand. A spoonful in their drink and they soon lost interest in anything but sleep.

'Whatever you say, Deputy. Will you tie off the sacks as I fill them? That way they'll be all ready when the sheriff comes for them.'

Foyle was glad to do it: anything to get the sheriff on the trail and out of town for a spell. Then he could relax . . .

But after the posse had at last gone off into the night and he began to relax, Deputy Foyle had no idea that when he woke up it would be full daylight — and that there would be no sign of Raina Redbird.

Only the ugly, foul-tempered assistant cook was there. She was a full-blood Lakota squaw with a huge dislike for white people. Which was probably why she clattered and banged the heavy iron cookware on the big

98

wood-burning range and made his throbbing head feel as if someone had split it with a tomahawk.

No, make that a full-size double-bitted lumber axe.

'Oh, Gawd! Lemme die before Bart gets back!'

6

Whetstones

Barton Gill had no intention of turning back before he ran Brett to earth. 'Brett' or 'Dan McCord', whoever the hell he was. No one made a fool of him by busting out of his jail, and, by hell, Deputy Foyle would find that out to his cost once the fugitive was back behind bars.

The men he had chosen for the posse were tough, hardened to the Dakota wilds in all weathers. He was confident he would run Brett down before the next sundown.

'By noon, if I have anythin' to do with it!' he gritted as they dismounted and led their horses up a steep, narrow winding trail in the foothills of the Whetstones.

'Come to think of it, Brett *must* be

Danny McCord!' Gill said aloud, startling the nearest two posse men. 'No one in their right mind would come in here unless he knew the Whetstones!'

'He was only a kid when he run out, weren't he, Bart?' one man asked and earned a bleak glare.

'A kid — reared by Big Al McCord, best frontiersman as ever rode this territory! Hell, they used to chase mavericks in these here foothills for the Arrowhead while Al was buildin' it up! He took a shine to that kid — at first, leastways. Took him everywhere with him, taught him all he knew. Yeah, that son of a bitch knows these hills, all right, an' he's gonna lead us one damn helluva chase before we nail him!'

The posse men exchanged glances, most were trying to hide their smiles: a prolonged manhunt meant the daily pay would climb up to a dollar, maybe even beyond.

Find yourself a good hidy-hole,

Danny boy! We ain't in that much of a hurry to catch up with you!

★ ★ ★

But Raina Redbird was in a hurry to find Brett.

She had managed to slip Foyle his Mickey Finn and then had dressed in buckskin trousers and overshirt, pulled her hair back and slipped on a headband. With a wide belt that held another knife in a beaded sheath and a .32 calibre Smith & Wesson pistol, she completed her outfit with her moccasin half-boots.

Easing through the shadows, she made her way to the old stables at the far end of the ground behind the rooming house and saddled her horse, a sleek, mostly grey, paint mustang with a sprinkling of blotches on the rump that might indicate appaloosa somewhere in its lineage.

There was a saddle-bag with food and ammunition for the carbine that

102

she took down from the rafters above the stable door. It was well wrapped in rawhide and oiled cloth and she slid it through the rawhide loop on her saddle.

Moments later she was a part of the night, slipping through the dark on the long-stretching grey pinto, the sharp wind feeling good against her face as she lifted it towards the stars.

This was the way she preferred to live, not confined to some whiteman-style house. She could put up with life as a boarding house proprietor as long as she had the pinto and the Whetstones to ride to on those rare occasions when there was free time to do so.

But this time was not as carefree as on the other occasions: this was serious business and she felt a strange compulsion to help this extraordinary man who called himself 'Brett' and who had come into her life almost before she had realized it.

She had regarded him as simply another roomer at first, then things had started to happen, chipping away the outer image, stirring something within her she could not put a name to.

All she wanted to do was help him accomplish whatever he had come to do. It frightened her a little, because she wasn't *sure* just what he was about.

But she knew there was some kind of vengeance behind it, which was maybe what stirred the blood of her ancestors that pounded through her veins.

★   ★   ★

In the early hours of the morning Belle McCord awoke from what she thought was a sound sleep and jerked upright in her bed.

She blinked in the dark room, hands clutching the sweaty sheets either side of her trim young body, feeling her heart pound and slam against her ribs.

There was something hammering at her brain. Blood was roaring in her ears. She felt totally disoriented, a queasiness in her stomach, which was all the more noticeable and alarming since Belle was a healthy young animal, never ill, never even caught a cold.

Dean, on the other hand, was always sniffling or coughing, drinking glasses of frothing bicarbonate of soda to 'settle' his stomach.

What was this affliction that had brought her out of a deep sleep with the suddenness of a gunshot?

Sweat was trickling from her hair over her damp temples and she sat there, forcing herself to take deep breaths, calming herself down, feeling her heart gradually return to its normal steady and strong *thump-thump! thump-thump!*

Then her eyes widened and her fingers clutched the sheet so tightly they almost tore the cloth.

With a small animal whine in her throat, she swung her legs out of bed, groped for her gown on the chair and hurriedly pulled it on. She was gasping again as she hurried to the door, accurately and confidently, through the dark.

She wrenched it open, letting it swing behind her, hurried along the passage, with its parquetry floor now hidden by the darkness, to her brother's room.

The door was unlocked and she burst in, calling his name, crossing to the bureau where she knew there was a china oil lamp. Dean was murmuring sleepily, starting to sit up when she struck a match and applied it to the wick. He squinted in the light.

'Belle! What in blazes . . . ?'

She stood beside the bed, holding her gown closed with one hand, pushing hair up out of her face with the other.

'*He's not Danny!*' she blurted. '*He can't be!*'

It took Dean a moment to realize what she was saying. Then he frowned, staring at her.

'Oh, Christ, sis! What the hell's this — in the middle of the night?'

She sat down on the bed, looking intently into his face. 'There was no birthmark!'

Dean blinked, his frown deepening, and he let out a deep breath. 'There were bandages on his back. It was probably covered up.'

'No! It would be higher than the bandages reached! They were only around his lower ribs. Dan's birthmark, that little blotch like a strawberry-coloured spider, should've been up near the top of his shoulder! You know that's where it was, Dean! Think!'

He held up a hand, confused. 'OK! You're right, but maybe we just missed it. I mean, we were looking at the scars from Pa's whipping — '

'He had *some* kind of scars! We didn't get a good enough look to say they were caused by a lash or — or something else.' She shook her head vigorously, hair spilling across her face again. 'No, Dean, he's *not* Danny!'

He digested this, then his mouth tightened.

'Then who the hell is he? And what's he doing up here?'

'I-I think he's here to — to get us!'

107

'What the hell does that mean: 'get us'?'

'I don't know. It's just that I feel he's here to . . . do us harm, Dean! He might even be going to . . . kill us!'

'He'll have a damn hard job doing that! Look, sis, you're overwrought and — '

'I am *not!*' Her small hands clenched down at her sides; he saw the set of her features now and knew this was no time to patronize her.

'Well, I can soon see he doesn't get near us. I'll send some men to help that fool Gill hunt this Brett down. They know the Whetstones better than those townsmen he's got for a posse.'

He flung back the bedclothes. She was smiling when she handed him his shirt from the chair.

'Tell them to take him alive if they can. I want to know who he is and why he's here. I'll look forward to finding out!'

★ ★ ★

108

These damn hills! They gave him the creeps.

Brett pushed the thought from him, but the fact was, he was a Plainsman. He liked to see ranges in the distance, blue-hazed, clawing up into the sky, and he liked being high up and looking out across country he aimed to cross.

But he never had liked timber growing so thickly that the trunks of trees brushed both a man's legs as his horse picked a way through. *Must be a hangover from the bad old days, when such places could hide enemies or just plain dollar-hungry bounty hunters after his scalp . . .*

But the same dense timber that made him uneasy was also his protection.

Hitting the Whetstones in the dark hadn't helped. There were landmarks to look for: the arrangememt of the peaks, how they looked as if they were the broken teeth of an inverted giant saw. Well, he was here to tell that it was mighty hard to see any kind of a pattern against the stars.

Not that the stars weren't bright; they were brighter than further south in his experience, but they seemed to have wider spaces between the clusters. And these blank spots were behind the range so he couldn't see the outline of the peaks clearly.

He broke out of the timber on to a high, rising trail that curved around a steep slope. Wind sawed like a knife-blade against his face, startling him; he hadn't realized how hot it was in amongst the trees. This Dakota Territory was a completely new experience for him, full of surprises and not all of them welcome.

He checked the roan and patted its neck as they both rested, the horse blowing some. It had been a hard, steep ride and he knew there was worse to come. He couldn't risk striking a match, so he would have to wait for first light before he could check the map he had stashed in the secret pocket near the bottom end of the leather rifle scabbard. He had stamped decorative leaves and checks around the area and amongst those designs were hidden the saddle-stitching that concealed the small pocket. It was one of the best hiding-places he knew of and it had served him well over the years.

There was no use stopping here: he could make out the flats below, a pale greyness against the blacker night, but there was no sign of a posse. Which meant nothing: they could have entered the Whetstones from any point. Barton Gill would know he would head here — where else was there for a fugitive to hide except in the Whetstones? Of course, he could have skirted the town and run for the south country with its vast flats carved up by deep canyons like the Staked Plains. But the lynch mob knew which direction he had taken, so Gill was bound to come to these hills in his search for him.

What he had to do was find his way to Gunbutt. Danny had told him it was the best place to hide out and he ought to know. He had used it after he had

111

clobbered Big Al and run for his life, going to ground there for almost a month before he dared make his way out and head south.

For a fifteen-year-old, he had showed a lot of spunk and know-how. When he had picked up the rumour, down near Deadwood, that Al McCord had died from his injuries, instead of panicking he had sat down with geological survey maps — he never did say where he had picked them up — worked out an escape route which took him through Cheyenne, then Denver and, eventually, all the way to Tucumcari, way down on the Canadian, or that section still called the Red River by some diehard Texans living in that part of New Mexico Territory.

'Yeah, you had it rough, kid,' Brett murmured as he started the roan for the curve in the trail, riding with his rifle across his thighs now. 'And a lot rougher was to come, but it'll all be squared away soon. You got my word on that.'

He was amongst some boulders, uncomfortable and mighty weary, when it became light enough to read. He pulled the rifle scabbard closer, felt around, counting the acanthus leaves on the design that encircled the base. Number four lifted easily with his fingernail. Then the clip it had protected gave him a little trouble before it came free. He opened the small flap, dug out the folded map. It was fairly thick but had been hidden well enough by the designs stamped into the leather pocket flap.

He frowned when he spread the creased sheet of paper, bringing it closer to his eyes in the grey light. It took him a few moments to find the section he wanted, though he was sure he had folded it in such a way that it would come close to hand after just unfolding the two outside sections.

It was pretty damn crude, the map, and the thick pencil lines had smeared some during the miles it had been carried in the rifle scabbard, all the way up from Amarillo.

He turned it this way and that, looking for landmarks and finding only one: a jutting ledge high above that wasn't actually part of the section called Gunbutt.

Brett froze as something up there moved. He prepared to roll towards his rifle, only an arm's length away, frowned when he saw the rider. *An Indian!* Buckskin-clad and holding a carbine which he now lifted above his head. Trying to attract attention! Now what the hell did that mean?

Then a voice drifted down to him:

'You're too far over! You must've missed the first trail — it's pretty well hidden by boulders and a stand of cedars. But come on up and I'll show you how to get to where you want to go.'

And how the hell would you know? he asked himself, recognizing Raina Redbird's voice.

114

7

Back

'I found your map.'

He looked at her sharply as they sat on the deadfall outside the shallow cave beneath a rocky ledge in the canyon. Shaped like a gunbutt and given that name because of it. She looked every part an Indian, only her slimness and the curves of her figure giving away the fact she was an Indian maiden and not a young warrior.

'Where'd you find it?' he demanded, perhaps more harshly than he intended.

'In your room, of course.' She gave him a tentative smile. 'After your fight in the stables, and with Barton Gill having you in jail, I thought I should learn more about this man who was living in one of my rooms and was so handy with his fists — and a gun.'

115

He felt his rising anger drain from him, nodded. 'Yeah, I guess . . . I'd been studying the map and, as I recollect, left it folded under my saddle-bags on the table. It was too thick to slip into the pocket on the rifle scabbard and I was trying to compress it. Danny drew it for me.'

Her gaze sharpened but she said, 'I recognized Gunbutt immediately. I've been here with my father and other Lakota children. It was a sort of *gathering* place where we could enjoy . . . nature, I suppose. Wildflowers and the animals that lived here, some you no longer see outside of these mountains. We called it *Oona-gazee*, a sheltered place.'

'Looks like it don't get used much these days.'

Her face was sad for a few moments. 'No. Our parents are dead and now we're adults in the world the white man has given us.' There was surprisingly little bitterness in her voice, but he asked quietly,

'You like to blame your bad luck or bad medicine or whatever you call it, on the white man?'

She shook her head. 'No. My mother was white, remember. And as you were at pains to tell me a little while back, there are good and bad in people of all races and colours. I try to remember that.'

He nodded. 'Why're you helping me?'

She was silent for a time, stirred the coals of the small fire where coffee was heating in Brett's battered pot.

'I'm not sure. Oh, the McCords are not likeable people. They have brought riches to the town and the county as a whole, but they are arrogant and at times bullying, especially Dean. They don't give me any custom. I feel I don't owe them anything.'

'Nor me.'

'No. Except I detect . . . something in you that . . . ' She looked directly at him. 'You would've made a good Indian.'

117

He laughed briefly. 'What makes you say that?'

'Something in your manner. You've come here for some purpose and you are not going to let anything stop you from doing it. My father was like that, dedicated; he would defy any odds once he decided on a course of action and if he felt the deed was important enough.'

'This is important — to me.'

'But it obviously involves a lot of other people.' She paused but he didn't say anything. 'I thought you *could* be Danny McCord returned to . . . straighten out a few things.'

'You'd've been pretty young when Danny left.'

'Yes, about eight or nine; he'd gone just before my mother and I arrived.' She stopped and gave him a sober look. 'Everyone was talking about how ungrateful he was, turning on Big Al McCord after he'd reared the boy. I think now you are not the young Dan McCord grown to adulthood.'

He shook his head. 'Danny's dead.'

She straightened on the log, frowning. Then she knelt and poured two tin mugs of the bubbling coffee. It was too hot to drink and they set it on the log to cool.

'I can't even begin to imagine why you are here, letting people think you are Danny McCord.'

'People can think what they like. Anyway, that was only the name Big Al gave him. He never knew his own name.'

'I'm intrigued.'

'Well, I guess you've a right to know.'

They took their coffee into the shade of the shallow cave. She produced a flour bag that held dried fruit, fresh biscuits, a small jar of Raina's blackberry jelly, even a pat of butter that was just starting to soften and run.

He drank half his coffee and rolled a cigarette.

'What about your name? This single word: 'Brett'?'

'That's my name, coincidence it was Molly McCord's maiden name. The

119

other part is 'Shannon', but I never knew my father.' He smiled wryly. 'Not sure my mother did, either. But she called me 'Brett' and that's good enough.'

'I didn't mean to pry that deep!'

He shrugged. 'Never mind me. Danny's story's much more interesting.'

★   ★   ★

Molly McCord's third child was still-born, a perfectly formed boy, strangled by the umbilical cord. It shattered her to the point where she would not even allow her husband to bury the body on Arrowhead land.

Big Al, tough, bareknuckle-brawling, gunfighting, bronc-busting Big Al McCord was a softy where Molly was concerned. He didn't argue, simply took that tiny body, wrapped tenderly in the shawl she had crocheted in readiness for his birth as far as his boundary. Then he rode for another day and a half before burying his second son beside a small mountain lake.

On the way back he came to a stageline swing station that served liquor and he got drunk. Next thing he knew he was riding with a search party, looking for a stage that was overdue. It turned out it had lost a wheel and replacing it had caused the delay. But they told of having heard shooting beyond the low range where they had come to grief. There had been smoke, too, a lot of smoke.

McCord and two others decided to take a look. They found a pilgrim wagon, burned out, the bodies of a family scattered about: a woman, two girl children, all three violated and scalped. Also a man and a boy, mutilated and scalped.

The trio were burying the victims when they heard a baby cry.

McCord shook his head vigorously, thinking he had drunk too much sourmash. But the crying didn't stop and eventually they opened a wooden box with a hinged lid that had somehow survived fire and the marauders. Inside, wrapped in a small blanket, was a boy child. McCord estimated him to be about a week old, no more.

He must have been travelling in the box and when the Indians attacked the parents must have hidden it, in the vain hope that the child would somehow survive, even if they didn't. It was one of those heart-rending decisions that many pioneers had to make.

The Indians must have been too occupied with their bloody deeds to have heard the baby crying.

Al took that baby back with him to Arrowhead but Molly refused to look at it, would have nothing to do with it. Just turned her face into her pillow and sobbed, body shaking.

Al McCord didn't know what to do. He couldn't sleep for the infant's constant crying, but then it stopped. Suddenly. Heart in mouth, he hurried to Molly's bedroom, afraid of what he would find.

She was sitting up in bed, the baby

boy at her breast, hungrily feeding on the milk her body had produced in readiness for the stillborn child. She smiled at her husband.

'We'll call him 'Daniel', after my dead brother.' She kissed the top of the small head. 'The Good Lord must've meant me to have this baby, not the other poor little mite.'

McCord had no belief in that sort of thing, but he had his wife back, that was all that mattered.

And because she doted so on the rescued child he soon forced himself to become openly fond of the boy, too. His eldest son, Dean, and the daughter, Belle, as children will, showed their resentment, pinching the child and upsetting him at every opportunity, while managing to look totally innocent themselves.

As the boy grew up and spent a lot of time in Big Al's company, the siblings' jealousy and resentment became more noticeable. Molly grew apart from her birth son and daughter, convinced that

123

God had sent Daniel as a special gift to her to nurture and love, and she showered all her affection upon him.

It wasn't long before Al himself began to feel pangs of jealousy, too. Molly had no time for anything or anyone; catering to the boy's every wish filled her entire life. He was even driven to visiting the girlie houses in town.

Then came the accident. Molly was thrown from a horse and broke her neck in a dry streambed.

Danny's life changed immediately — for the worst. He was, by now, almost ten years old, had been spoiled by Molly, found it mighty hard to adjust to the rough-and-ready spartan ways Big Al, Dean and Belle forced upon him. He must've felt lost, as if he were starting another life — one he had no liking for. He ran away a few times but was always found easily enough; a doctor opined that the boy *wanted* to be found. It was his way of getting attention.

Al told him more than once he was

sorry he had rescued him from that wagon massacre. Although it must have hurt badly, it also drove the boy into trying harder at everything he did, seeking Big Al's approval, trying to impress him and show he *was* worthy of the McCord name.

Then Al had an abrupt reversal of his feelings: he discovered the boy was a natural horseman. He had a special kind of rapport with horses, could ride easily where others had to fight their mounts or give up. He could track well and was a good shot with a rifle. These were attributes admired by Al McCord; he had always lamented the fact that Dean, although eager enough, was not much of a cattleman.

Dean's resentment of Danny turned to open hatred and the pair had several knock-down-drag-out fights. Once Dean beat the younger boy with an axe handle, breaking one of his arms. Al punished Dean harshly: sent him out with his roughest men to gather mustangs for the remuda, made him participate in the castration of stallions and bulls. He forced him to do every dirty, undesirable chore that everyone else shied away from: cleaning out the tick dip-tank, mucking out the stables, digging a new sanitary pit after filling in the old one.

Naturally, Dean's resentment and hatred for Danny increased. And Belle backed her brother up; they could both see that if he kept impressing Big Al the boy would inherit a major share of Arrowhead when Big Al died.

And then, as the years passed and Dan grew into his teens, as capable as any of the adult cowhands, Al decided the boy was ready for the responsibility of driving a herd of prime cows to the stock agent, Bob Dalby, in town twelve miles away. Three men went with him, chosen by Dean.

Somehow, the herd was sold for a paltry sum, through Dig Latham, another friend of Dean's, one of Dalby's employees. Then it was quickly sold again to a trail herder for a massive profit.

The theft — for it was nothing else — was soon discovered. Dan claimed he couldn't remember signing anything. Latham had enticed him to have a snifter of whiskey and Dan reckoned Bob Dalby or one of his men must've put something in the drink so that he didn't know what he was doing. Dalby, an old and, up till then, a trusted friend of the McCords, naturally denied the allegation, produced witnesses who said they'd seen Dan sign the consent form of his own accord.

Later, these same witnesses, the Arrowhead cowhands, overheard him threaten the stock agent when Dalby refused to pay him a commission he felt he was entitled to.

Somehow Dalby convinced Big Al that it had been all Dan's idea and he knew nothing about it; his own man, Latham, had set it up and had now disappeared with much of the money, leaving Dan to try to explain.

It wasn't until much later that it was learned that Dean and Belle had played their part in the framing of young Dan.

Al raged at Danny for what he, naturally, saw as a terrible betrayal. Dean and Belle reinforced this by reminding their father they had told him long ago that Dan was only biding his time to take whatever he could from Arrowhead. The boy was worthless in their opinion. Big Al was angry enough — and hurt enough — to listen and agree.

Danny tried to make a run for it, was caught by some of Al's hardcases and given a beating on Dean's orders, then literally dragged back to Arrowhead.

Big Al had taken a whip to the boy, who had fought back, wrenched up a fence post and smashed it across Al's head.

He was saddling his horse to quit Arrowhead when Belle and Dean came in, both visibly upset, and told him Al was not expected to live through the night. They urged him to leave unless he wanted to face a murder charge.

This was the story most of the county knew, but . . .

The frightened fifteen-year-old had, of course, run. A long time later he came across Dig Latham who was down on his luck and, for the price of a few drinks and a decent feed, Danny learned the truth.

★ ★ ★

Raina waited but Brett said no more right then. She nodded.

'We heard bits and pieces of the incident but not all the details. It was always suspected that Dean and Belle had engineered the whole thing with Bob Dalby and framed Danny, just to get rid of him and make sure he was disinherited.' She poured more coffee and it was cool enough to sip right away. 'Where do you come into it, Brett?'

'Not till just a few years ago,' he said quietly, his mind going back, remembering. 'I didn't meet Danny until he was in his twenties. And a long way from here.'

129

8

Buckshot

The big trouble started south of Cheyenne.

Brett had been riding the knife edge for way too long, stepping over into lawlessness, then, when driven back — usually not too far ahead of a posse — he told himself: *That's it! No more trying to dodge lawmen's bullets.* He wasn't yet closing in on his thirties and here he already had a strand or two of grey showing in his dark hair.

But once safe and sound again and with empty pockets and belly to match, it was easy enough to make for one of the many scattered hideaways and see if some of the old bunch might be there.

Usually there was someone he knew, and there would be an express box that needed 'liberating' from a Wells Fargo stage, or a railroad paychest, even some plump steers on a trail herd not far away and bound for the market in Cheyenne.

He knew it was his own fault, returning to these same holes in the wall, but what could a man do when he was alone, low on ammunition, cash and grub?

A quick solution to such problems was the only real answer, and if it meant taking a few risks — OK!

'Hell, I been taking risks one way and another since I busted outta the orphanage when I was twelve years old.'

That was no justification of course, but the fact was that, after running away, he had fallen in with a likeable rogue calling himself 'Applejack'. He put Brett to good use, dressed him in rags (even worse than the ones he was wearing), dirtied him up some more and then rubbed his bottom eyelids, on the outside, with wild onion. The tears flowed, filled the eyes and reddened them.

He was a mighty sorry-looking waif when he knocked on the doors of better-than-average houses and, sniffling, begged a meal. It worked every time, for Brett was a fine little actor. A quick grab at the table silver or a few coins stashed in a biscuit barrel and he was away. A full belly was his reward; the hard cash and silverware — and any strong liquor he was able to lay his hands on — went to Applejack.

Brett was satisfied with just being fed well: something he had never experienced at the orphanage. Applejack seemed to exist on a minimum of food, but fortified himself with hard liquor.

There were times when things backfired and they both did a stretch or two in local jails. Brett used his acting ability so well that he was more than once released early.

The parting with Applejack came one stormy night when a man named Franklin rode out of the rain and hunkered down by their campfire. He was a sullen man, bewhiskered and without even a cornsack to protect his shoulders from the driving rain. His six-gun was wet, but it worked well enough when Franklin suddenly drew it and shot Applejack between the eyes.

'What'd you do that for?' piped Brett, horrified.

'Reminded me of a Bible-bangin' brother-in-law I once had. Couldn't stand the son of a bitch. Don't worry, kid. I'll take care of you.'

'Not me!' Brett threw himself into the darkness of the storm. The gun triggered several times but he made it clear and kept going over the mountain, ending up on the edge of a trail camp where he was taken in and fed and then put to work.

That was his first experience of trail driving and he took to it like a duck to a pond. He found he could work horses by instinct: he had sure had no experience with them prior to this. He liked the work, stayed with the trail boss, the later famous 'Denver Digby', for three years. Digby was a rough old

133

cob, took that boy and turned him into a man; taught him how to ride fast and safely, how to shoot six-gun and rifle, gave him know-how about cattle, how to live off the land as well as any Indian born to the chore.

'One thing I can't teach you, boy, is honour. Now that don't necessarily mean 'honesty' in the sense that a body has to follow the letter of the law and dot his i's and cross his t's. He could be a renegade with the biggest bounty in the territory on his head, but if he had his own code of honour and stuck to it, he could feel proud, no matter what his crimes.'

'I don't get it, Digby.'

'It's easy, boy. You give your word, you keep it. You say you'll be someplace at a certain time, you bust a gut to get there. You see some wrongdoin' and some meek ol' citizen, or a member of the fairer sex, is in trouble, you don't walk away — not without doin' your damnedest to set the matter to rights. You savvy that?'

134

Brett thought about it. 'Even if it means tackling the son of a bitch makin' the trouble?'

'*Specially* tacklin' the son of a bitch that makes the trouble. You go for him with fists or guns.'

Brett frowned. 'I might not be as good a fighter!'

'So? There's only one way to find out — and you take it, or you ain't no man I want in my crew.'

'Jeepers! That's risky livin'!'

'It's a *man*'s way of livin', Brett. Risky, yeah. But any decent man is duty-bound to help someone he sees needs it. Now, you gotta find the wherewithal to do that within yourself. No one can give it to you.' The old trail driver leaned forward and drove a stiffened finger into the boy's chest, sending him staggering. 'It comes from in there. I figure you won't have no trouble findin' it, Brett. I can read a man pretty well an' you'll shape up good.'

Brett was somewhat daunted by the

135

high standard Digby had set him, and yet it came easily enough. He didn't even stop to think the first time he saw some young woman being rough-handled by a red-faced man in a big hat.

He was a deal smaller than the man, but he was wearing a gun, and when he couldn't pull the man off, he used his Colt to knock him off his feet. The girl screamed and, startling him, slapped his face and pushed him away, hurrying to the dazed man, who was now sitting up in the dust.

'You leave my father alone, you dirty little trail kid!'

'I-I — he was whuppin' you!'

'He's my *father*! He had the right!' She knelt beside the dazed man, wiping a trickle of blood from the stubbled face with her handkerchief. 'It's all right, Poppa. I-I won't see Randy Jenks no more, if you don't want me to.' She glared at the stunned Brett. 'You better git, before he comes round proper! Or he'll whup *you* good!'

Denver Digby — and half the trail camp — laughed uproariously when Brett, quite indignantly, told them of the incident.

'You gotta take the bad with the good, kid.'

'How can I tell when not to butt in?'

'You'll know. It'll come to you.'

And it did. Except for the time the leader of a bunch of Kansan farmers wanted to hit the herd with a bounty of a dollar a head to allow them to cross their farmlands. 'It's a tick levy on your lousy Texas longhorns.'

The man sounded reasonable at first. He had tough but regular features. The men backing him looked mean and were heavily armed. Brett had ridden out with Digby ahead of the herd, now driving in slowly a mile or two behind, looking for sundown water.

Digby, of course, argued, protested, in the end flatly refused to pay. Then suddenly the mild-mannered man was mild-mannered no more.

'Then die, you tick-ridden Texas

bastard!' he snapped, and shot Digby through the chest.

Brett was stunned, horrified. They paid him no attention, him being not much more than a kid, until, recovering, shaking inside but appearing quite calm and cool outwardly, he said,

'You murderin' son of a bitch! Throw that rifle down! I'm takin' you in to the law in Abilene!'

The men guffawed, but stopped abruptly when Miles lifted his rifle, his intentions plain. Suddenly the kid's Colt was in his hand, blazing twice. His lead punched the Kansan out of the saddle, setting his horse to rearing and stomping. The rest were stunned, then the nearest lifted his shotgun, snarling, 'You goddamn murderin' little bastard!'

Brett shot him out of the saddle, too, though it wasn't a fatal wound. But it made the others scatter, gave him time to grab the reins of Digby's horse, upon which the trail driver was sagging in the saddle, taking his dying breaths.

He rode off and was over the rise

before they started shooting and came after him.

But the trail men had heard the guns and the Kansans fell back when they saw the hard-eyed Texans riding in with rifles catching the sunlight.

They buried Digby and the trail boss, Martin Kelso, said, 'You done good, Brett.'

'Not good enough. I had a hunch that Miles was only puttin' on a friendly front, but I never butted in as early as I oughta in case I was wrong.'

'You done good,' Kelso repeated. 'Boys, the herd ain't yet settled for the night. I think this calls for a little overtime. Like a stampede through that long wire fence them Kansans have strung . . .'

And that was how that particular herd got to Abilene on time and filled the pens to bursting point.

Brett was different after that drive. Harder. More grown up. He practised long and hard with his six-gun, not looking for more gunfights, but half-afraid that someone might come to

139

square with him on behalf of Miles. He had sweaty dreams about the killing for weeks afterwards, thoughts about it for a lot longer, coming at odd, unbidden times.

The cattle trails were his home for years. He had other gunfights and fist-fights, but he never forgot what Denver Digby had taught him: he tried to keep his honour at all costs. Then there was a gunfight in Socorro. He downed his man, an arrogant young flashy, in the small sun-burned plaza. They were to draw on the drop of a kerchief, but the man with the cloth gave the flashy a nod and he went for his gun before the kerchief fluttered groundward. It didn't do him any good: Brett shot him twice before the Colt cleared leather. Unfortunately, there were three more brothers whom Brett didn't know about — and one was the local sheriff.

So, the first Wanted dodger with his name on it was posted along all the cattle trails and in frontier towns. He was branded an outlaw and a thief; the dead man's brothers claimed he was part of a gang who had robbed the Wells Fargo depot in the next town along, and the dead brother had been trying to arrest him when he was shot down.

Keeping to little-known trails, Brett eventually joined up with a bunch of hardcases. It turned out that *these* were the men who had robbed that Fargo depot.

'Well, hell, kid, welcome to the outfit,' chuckled the red-bearded leader, Brick Radkin. 'Might as well come join us, seein' you're already branded as one of us.'

By then Brett had had enough of dodging posses and bounty hunters all on his own, so he was ready for Radkin's Raiders, as the bunch was called. Brick had been a guerrilla fighter for the South during the war and most of this bunch were men who had fought under his leadership. They had spent more time looting civilian warehouses

141

and riverboats than raiding Yankee columns; they found it hard to stop after Armistice.

'God!' Brett said, surprised. 'War's been over ten years!'

'An' we still got mostly men of the original Raiders,' Radkin said proudly. 'Glad to have you with us, Brett. Stick, and we'll make you rich.'

Brett wondered why the others weren't already rich, after ten years of outlawry under Radkin's leadership.

He enjoyed the danger, though, even the chases for a long time, till Radkin was severely wounded and had to be taken to a large town where there was a good doctor. There they were recognized by local law and forced to scatter.

Travelling the wild trails, which were the only ones he knew now, Brett soon fell in with other gangs and in one of them, in Missouri, he met Danny McCord; they hit it off right away.

Danny was a little younger than Brett, a quiet man, with a haunted look. Brett saw the scars on his back one time when they were washing in a river, totally naked, scrubbing dirt from their flesh with handfuls of sand.

'Them scars look hard-earned, Danny.'

Danny snapped his head around, then nodded jerkily. 'They're why I'm here with this ignorant bunch . . . present company excepted, o'course!'

'Yeah,' Brett said, looking at the dirty, bedraggled men they had been riding with, now sprawled along the riverbank. He could see that Danny didn't want to discuss the scars. 'Reckon we can do better without tryin' too hard.'

'Just ride on out?'

Brett doubted that would work. These were mean bastards: had been held together well enough when they had first been joined by a man calling himself the Colonel, but he had been shot off a high trail two months back and the man who had taken over, Dal Hunnicutt, was as mean as they come and a boozer to boot. He also figured he was a lot smarter than he really was.

They hadn't pulled a successful job

143

since he had taken over. His planning was scatterbrained but he was the type who resented having his short-comings pointed out; one man had tried it and Hunnicutt tossed him through a window. The glass slashed the carotid artery and the man had bled to death. No one could be sure whether Hunnicutt meant it to happen or not.

'There has to be a challenge,' Brett said as they dried off on the grass in the warm sun, some distance from the others.

Danny looked at him sharply. 'You up to that?'

Brett shrugged. 'I dunno. I don't want to lead this crew, but I don't want Dal Hunnicutt doing it, neither.'

'Why don't we just ride out after they're asleep?'

'They'll come after us.'

'So?'

Brett arched his eyebrows. 'You up to *that*?'

He had never seen Danny get his gun out really fast: there had been no occasion to, when he thought about it. Mostly it was take your time and check your guns before going in to steal an express box or mailbag or valise of money.

If there was any shooting — and there usually was — the guns were already out before it started.

Now Danny McCord told him: 'I can shoot the eye out of a squirrel at fifty yards, and Dal Hunnicutt's a mighty lot bigger'n any squirrel I ever saw.'

Brett nodded slowly. 'Keep it at long range, huh? Reckon that'd be best.' He smiled a little, adding, 'I'm not too bad with a rifle, either.'

★ ★ ★

The opportunity came after yet another job went wrong and the gang had to hightail it with lead whistling about their ears. There had been a posse waiting between two buildings on the edge of the town; the idea was for the men who had waited in ambush near

145

the bank to drive the renegades down towards the waiting posse. It didn't work.

Three riders spurred that way, ran into a wall of lead and itchy trigger fingers. They went down, with their dying mounts thrashing around them.

Hunnicutt instantly wheeled his mount down an alley and most of the others followed, but Danny McCord signalled frantically until he caught Brett's attention. They veered away, dropped back and left town by the road that led to the stockyards. The pens were full of bawling cattle when they realized that there were more posse men coming their way. Someone must've tipped off the local law! Likely because the reward had been lifted to just short of $3,000 now.

They weren't going to make it, that was clear. But both seemed to have the same idea at the same time; each spurred towards a pen, leaned swiftly from the saddle, with lead chewing splinters from the rails, and swung open

146

the gates. A couple of shots close to the nearest steers was all it took.

The renegades wheeled aside as the line, quickly spreading wide, surged and tumbled and bawled its way out of the pens. The nearest way out for the fear-driven cattle was up the side street which was almost blocked by deputies. Not for long!

There was a wild milling and yelling, lots of gunshots, which swiftly faded as Brett and Danny raced their mounts around the pens and lit out for the wide open plains.

Three days later they ended up in a canyon shaped like a harp. They could still grin when they thought about the way those so-called deputies had panicked when they saw that wave of wild-eyed longhorns heading for them, like a herd straight out of hell.

Relaxed now, and deciding this was the time to cut loose of Hunnicutt's gang of losers, they made camp on the coarse sand surrounding a couple of waterholes. One had a dead deer and a chipmunk decomposing at the edge so they were leery about using water from the other hole but it was clear and tasted sweet. To be on the safe side, they boiled a couple of cansful first before brewing the last of their coffee, which smelled great.

They washed down most of their remaining jerky with the brew.

The only thing was, the appetizing odour of that coffee drifted through the strangely shaped canyon on the afternoon breeze. Before sundown, Dal Hunnicutt was there with his two surviving gang members. Quietly, they took up their positions among rocks which afforded them shelter but allowed them to look down upon the camp near the waterholes.

'That coffee sure smells good — too good for a pair of snakes like you!'

At the first words yelled by Hunnicutt — a fool to the end, giving warning instead of shooting — Danny and Brett scooped up their rifles from the sand and dived in different directions,

148

splitting the target. They had already picked out rocks close by where they would hole up if just this kind of situation developed.

Brett hurled himself headlong for his low ribbon of rock, twisting in mid-air when he saw Tully standing atop his own boulder so as to have a better shot. The killer jerked and flung his rifle high in reflex as the lead punched into his body. Tully's rifle went off in mid-air, spun wildly with the recoil and clattered on to the ledge where Hunnicutt crouched.

The outlaw boss dropped flat just as Danny fired and the bullet passed overhead, but ricocheted, making him dig his fingers so hard into the rock that his nails splintered.

Danny spun the other way as soon as he saw Hunnicutt drop, lever working. Bateman, the second outlaw, was on one knee, drawing bead, when Brett's slug took him in the head.

As McCord dropped back a shotgun roared and he heard the whistle of the buckshot overhead.

He saw Brett stagger, take a lunging step towards his cover. But he tripped on a rock poking up a few inches through the coarse sand. He went down, losing his rifle, the back of his shirt in tatters and blood spreading.

Danny yelled his name and leaped over his own protective barrier.

He slid in the loose sand, staggered, and came into a crouch between the wounded Brett, who was floundering weakly, trying to reach his rifle, and Hunnicut's shotgun as the outlaw leader stood, sighted down the barrel, and fired.

Danny dropped to one knee and worked lever and trigger in a blur of speed. The sounds of the three shots he got off were drowned in the thunder of the shotgun's second barrel. McCord was flung back a yard and a half as the charge of buckshot hit him. He went down hard, in a welter of blood.

Hunnicutt had been hurled violently back to land between two rocks, head at a very odd angle. Not that it mattered.

There were two blood-spurting holes in his chest.

The third bullet had torn his throat out.

9

Don't let me down!

'So that was how Danny McCord died?'

Raina Redbird had been about to say more but Brett soberly shook his head. His voice was flat, deliberately devoid of any sign of emotion.

'No. He took a lot longer to die.'

She frowned as he stood and looked around the canyon, checked the skyline once more.

'But you said he was blasted with a shotgun by that man Hunnicutt — and you were, too!'

'My wound wasn't all that serious. The buckshot raked my back as I fell, gouged a few criss-cross lines from my shoulder out towards my ribs. I hit my head on a rock — that's what put me out of action.'

He lifted his long hair above his left temple and she saw the puckered, two-inch-long scar there.

'The buckshot left those scars on your upper back? The ones that look like someone has whipped you?'

He nodded. 'Danny was all busted up by the charge he'd taken in the chest — the one that was meant for me.'

Raina's gaze sharpened; there was a strange tone in his voice.

'Danny saved my life, Raina.'

She nodded slowly: he was the kind of man who would see it that way.

She was beginning to see just why Brett was here now, given the kind of man he was showing himself to be.

'I came round, and apart from being a little weak from loss of blood and the head wound, I was OK, though I wasn't seeing too clearly. Danny was breathing but he was a mess. His left arm was hanging by a shred and one eye . . . '

He stopped as she lifted a hand. 'I — don't need a detailed description.'

'Sorry. I managed to make a *travois*. I

knew how — we used 'em plenty of times on the trail drives, for carrying extra gear as well as hurt men. I found a way out of the canyon and it took me clear through those mountains. Luckily the posses were all hunting on the other side. I made for a town on the Sabine River where I knew a doctor, a man good at his trade — you hear about these things when trail-driving and never know when you'll need a good sawbones. I waited till dark before I took Danny in . . . '

* * *

The medico, Doctor Swann, worked for two hours on Danny before Brett would agree to him treating his own wounds. By that time he had lost a good deal of blood and was almost out on his feet, feeling nauseated, his vision blurred.

'Obviously concussion,' opined Swann in a no-nonsense tone. 'You'll need rest, too.'

Despite Brett's protests Swann patched

154

him up, stitching the head gash, and put him in a bed near Danny.

'Is he gonna live, Doc?'

Swann, a tall, cadaverous man with a friendly face and small goatee, stared down at Brett for what seemed like a long minute.

'He might. But if he does, he'll be an invalid. I'll have to amputate that left arm before morning. One lung is partially collapsed; I won't answer for the condition of his heart, and, unfortunately, he'll have to lose that eye. Also, there're buckshot lodged against his spine. I dare not touch them — if I nicked the spinal cord trying to pick the shot out, he might never walk again. As it is, he'll find it quite . . . difficult.'

Brett stayed around until Danny regained consciousness two days later. Swann didn't mince words and Danny stared at his empty sleeve, straining his head to see the stump bound in bloody bandages; his one remaining eye was on the other side of his face which made it awkward. He looked up at Swann and Brett.

'I — won't be a burden — to no man.'

'Don't be foolish, boy!' the sawbones snapped. 'You've got your legs, one arm, one eye. Sure, folk'll stare at you, just as they did when mutilated soldiers came back from the war. They'll feel sorry for you and that might be the hardest thing of all to live with, but it can be done. There're places where folk with all kinds of crippling injuries can be trained to live as normal and productive a life as possible.'

'It's the 'as possible' that don't attract me, Doc.' Danny gasped. It was an obvious effort for him to speak. He flicked his single eye from Swann to Brett. 'Doc — I — need to see — Brett — a — alone.'

Swann agreed readily enough and left. Brett felt a little uneasy at being alone with someone injured so terribly. Danny lifted his right hand.

'Brett, you don't owe — me — nothin' . . . '

'Apart from my life.'

The fingers flicked and managed to convey Danny's annoyance. Brett realized just how hard it was for him to talk and decided not to interrupt, to let Danny have his say.

'I — went renegade to — to get me a — quick stake.' He made a brief sound that was a cross between a grunt and a derisive laugh. 'Somethin' else that — din' work out for — me.' His breathing was noisy and obviously painful but his one eye glared when Brett suggested he leave off for a spell, talk later. 'Needed — *money* — I — I got some squarin'-away — to be done. Big-time.' He grunted and lifted his hand, pointing shakily at himself. 'Kinda — handicapped now. Will you — help me?' Brett started to speak but Danny moved his head a little, side to side. 'W-wait — have to tell you — it'll mean goin' up agin — the Mc — McCords.'

Brett squeezed the limp hand.

157

'Whoever it is, Danny, and whatever you want done, just tell me and I'll do it.'

The pale mutilated lips moved, one side kind of sagging. Brett swore under his breath as he realized this was as much of a smile as Danny would ever be able to give.

* * *

Raina busied herself getting the camp things together while Brett smoked silently, sitting on a rock, nursing his rifle, remembering those terrible days at Danny McCord's bedside.

She, like most folk hereabouts, knew how Danny had been found as a baby in the hinged box at the site of his family's massacre and how Big Al had taken him back and given him to the depressed Molly. She frowned and spoke quietly.

'If Danny was contemplating . . . destroying the McCords . . . I-I don't understand. I mean, they raised him

158

when he could've died in that wagon box. Oh, I know he had a rough time with Al and Dean and Belle after Molly died, but from what I know, Danny seems to have shaped up into a pretty good sort of . . . human being.'

'For a whiteman, eh?' He smiled crookedly and quickly lifted a hand as she bristled. 'Sorry. Trying to be smart. No, it wasn't anything the McCords had done while raising him. He could've lived with those easily, likely didn't even hold a grudge once he was free of them.'

Her frown deepened. 'Then . . . what? And you seemed ready to do whatever he wanted — without even knowing why!'

He shrugged, a bit uneasily. 'The man'd saved my life. He was smashed up, dying a little at a time, depressed. He needed to know that someone would stand by him, do what he was no longer capable of doing himself.'

'And you — might've changed your mind after he . . . died?'

His face hardened, startling her. 'Not by a damn sight! I gave him my word and I aim to keep it!'

She felt tight in the chest, seeing that hard-bitten, obstinate face. Raina decided to hold her peace and let him tell it his way.

'Danny had always been troubled by the fact that he knew nothing about his family, except that once Al McCord mentioned there had been a lot of prospecting gear at the wagon site, so his father had probably been a prospector. After he ran off from Big Al, and they'd stopped looking for him, he found out that the wagon had likely come from a place called Rushaway. You heard of it?'

'Yes. Twenty, thirty years ago it was gold-rush country, but petered out. It's been a ghost town for years.'

He saw her face change as the significance struck her. 'Danny's father had found gold at Rushaway?'

'Seems that way. Hit it big, kept it to himself, but, like all those places, word

160

got around. Danny went there, found nothing but a few diehards trying their luck, moved on as his wanderings took him places he could make a living. But something kept pulling him back to Rushaway. It was no more than a ghost town, but there were still all the old records, abandoned along with most other things when the gold ran out and the population moved on. Just walked away.'

He paused and rolled another cigarette and she noted how grim his face was. 'He checked through those records of mining licences and so on, and found a name he knew.'

'My God!' Her hand fluttered up near her mouth. 'Don't — don't tell me it was Al McCord's!'

He nodded. 'There was a crippled oldster still living there, who made himself a few dollars by telling travellers about Rushaway's heyday — the fights, murders, bonanzas, and so on. Likely made most of them up or embellished a few incidents beyond recognition. But

161

the old feller, called Hoppy because of his twisted leg, listened mighty closely when Danny told his story, hoping Hoppy might recall the family.'

Raina Redbird waited, lips slightly parted, a glint of expectation in those dark, searching eyes.

'To cut it short,' Brett said suddenly, gruffly, 'Hoppy did recall them, but only knew the man who must've been Danny's father by the name of Buck. Some said it was short for Starbuck but there was no Starbuck in the old mine record book.'

'But there was a 'McCord'?'

'Yeah. Al McCord. Seemed he used to appear on the Rushaway field every so often. Looking for a little gold to help get his ranch started, I guess. But one time he brought along two hardcase pards, and one of them crippled old Hoppy by throwing him down a mineshaft and stealing the little gold he'd dug. McCord's bunch had a reputation as claim-jumpers. But Buck and his family suddenly upped stakes, loaded their wagon and moved out one night. That sort of thing was a dead giveaway, of course.'

'You mean they'd found gold?'

'According to Hoppy, Buck'd hit a rich vein. Danny's mother was pretty heavily pregnant, with *him*, I guess, and Buck'd decided it was a good time to pull out. Shortly after, McCord and his pards left and went after Buck's wagon.'

He stopped speaking and when she continued to look expectantly at him, he spread his hands.

'Yeah. Just what you're thinking; McCord and his gang hit the wagon, made it look like an Indian massacre.'

'I feel . . . sick! But — the baby? Danny . . . ?'

He shrugged. 'Must've been as Al told it. Molly'd lost her baby and he took Danny as a replacement. I wouldn't know his motives. Seems his mind had more twists than a stick of barleysugar candy. His two pards were found dead in a gulch not far from the wagon; there'd been a fight, probably over the gold. And it was Danny's father's gold. Al used it to build Arrowhead. *That*'s why Danny wanted to see the McCords wiped out.'

She nodded slowly. 'I'm beginning to understand.'

'Too bad someone got to Big Al first. I'd've enjoyed killing that snake.'

'If it's true, he did a terrible thing, but Al McCord did some good things, too, for the county here, helped a few folk down on their luck.'

'Guilty conscience. Likely why he turned on Danny. The boy would've been a constant reminder of what he'd done, so he treated him rough, hoping he'd quit. Otherwise he might've ended up killing him — which would've been mighty hard to explain away.'

'You're probably right. And now, although you're a fugitive, you are going after Belle and Dean?'

'I gave my word to Danny.'

'But they're almost innocent bystanders, aren't they? They had nothing to do

164

with stealing the gold.'

'You see 'em that way? They hated Danny. Mebbe they even knew it was rightfully his gold that built their ranch and made 'em rich. Al seems to've had some kind of conscience. Dean and Belle treated Danny like dirt. You find anything likeable about them two?'

'Not much, I have to admit. Just the same — '

'They're Arrowhead,' he cut in bluntly. 'Danny fought like hell before the end there, gave me every detail he could remember about the McCords and the ranch, the folks they dealt with in town and so on. I felt like I'd lived through those years with him.'

'Was it his idea that you should let them think you were Danny grown up?'

'No. That just happened when Rowley thought he recognized me from somewhere. Might've even been on an old Wanted dodger. Once he realized I knew a lot about the McCords he tried to tie me in with Danny. I'm obliged for

165

your help, Raina, but I'll handle it from here on in.'

'You can live with that?'

'You don't believe it, stick around and see for yourself.'

Her teeth tugged at her bottom lip. She watched him check his gear, wiping dust and grit carefully from his guns, rubbing them with an old oily cloth. He heard her small grunt of surprise.

'I call it 'house cleaning'. Might seem fussy but when you've travelled as many trails as I have, with someone behind you who only wants your carcase so they can collect the bounty, you don't take any chances.'

'It must be a — a very stressful kind of life you lead.' When he didn't answer she asked, 'How long did Danny live?'

His head snapped up and she felt uneasy under his bleak stare. 'Long enough to tell me all I need to know. His last words to me were, 'Don't let me down'. I don't aim to.'

★ ★ ★

166

Dean McCord buckled on the gunbelt and looked at his grim-faced sister. 'You check all the guns?'

'Every last one — for the fifth time!'

'All right, all right. It's not you ridin' out to go after that damn killer. Listen, give me Pa's old shotgun. It's awkward to carry with the long barrel but it's a damn sight more accurate than the sawed-offs. Rackman and the others can take them if they want.'

'You'll have enough guns to start a war.'

'I aim to finish one!'

'One we didn't realize was still going on.'

He nodded, tense, settled his gun belt again, took out the Colt one last time and checked the loads. Belle made an exasperated sound and left the room. When she came back with Big Al's old Purvis shotgun she held up the square shellbox and shook it. It rattled and he frowned.

'How many?'

'Only four.'

'Christ! And it's that fancy Limey calibre. No spares — which you could've ordered!'

'I think you talk just to hear the sound of your own voice at times, Dean.'

'Aw, go to hell!'

'Don't *you*!' she retorted as he stomped towards the door.

He paused, looked back, his face softening some. 'Sorry, sis. I'm all keyed up. Wasn't expecting to have to go after Danny ever again.'

'You really think he *is* Danny?'

'Aw, I dunno. Whoever he is, he must've been with Danny, even if he ain't the kid himself grown up. He knows too damn much not to've talked with him.'

'You think he knows about the gold? I mean, what Pa told us about 'finding' it with the baby in that box. It never did sit quite easy with me.'

He frowned. 'Don't start that again. If Pa *did* steal it, even if he arranged that 'massacre', it's nothin' to do with us.'

'How can you say that?' Her face was

pale and he knew she had been thinking about this subject a lot more than she had admitted to. 'It has everything to do us! It gave us this ranch, how we grew up, decent clothes and food and education. Well, I had more than you, but Pa gave you some schooling, too. It was only that he needed you on the ranch that he brought you back here so soon.'

'Pa give me my education *here*, on Arrowhead! It's the only schoolin' I was interested in. And I don't aim to sit back and let this Brett, whoever he is, take Arrowhead away from me.'

Her teeth tugged at her lower lip. 'D'you think Brett killed Pa?'

'I dunno; could've. I had a notion it was mebbe one of them nesters downstream. Pa did some bottom-of-the-deck dealing with them when he was buying 'em out. Strange Brett turnin' up the day Pa was buried, though. But, no matter. *He*'s a dead man, even if he don't know it yet.' Hand on the doorknob, he spoke over his shoulder. 'And I won't be back until he is.'

10

Shoot on Sight!

Sheriff Barton Gill's posse was lost.

This was what happened when a sheriff rarely left the town precincts, sending deputies on any chore that required riding out into the surrounding country. He had left Deputy Floyd back in town, in a fit of pique with the clumsy man, and now wished he hadn't.

Floyd knew the country pretty well, having ridden to most parts of the basin. Maybe he didn't know the Whetstones all *that* well, but his knowledge of them had to be better than Barton Gill's.

The sheriff had pinned his faith in the latest geological survey map to reach his office, but realized too late that the Whetstones themselves hadn't been surveyed. The country surounding them had, because this was land being made available for settlement. But although there was talk of building a road across the lowest section of range, utilizing the narrow pass known as Coffeebean, nothing had yet been approved by the Territorial Government, so no survey had been undertaken.

'Send someone back for Floyd, Bart,' suggested one of the posse, a big-muscled, tobacco-chewing townsman from the general store, name of Watkins — Watty to his friends. 'We're only chasin' our own asses this way.'

Gill glared, angry with himself, but not about to be told he was a damn fool by some storeman who had so many muscles from loading and unloading that they had squeezed his brain down to something about the size of a duck egg . . . make that a *chicken* egg, a *small* chicken.

'You want to go fetch Floyd?' the sheriff snapped. 'I'll send you, OK, but

171

your deputy pay stops till you get back. Be half a day, I calc'late.'

Watty spat a stream of tobacco. 'Jus' tryin' to be helpful, Bart! No need to turn bitchy.'

Gill snorted and returned to the map again, knowing he wasn't going to get anywhere.

'Anyways, Bart,' spoke up another man, Bradley, oldest in the group, wheezing. 'Reckon this tells us Brett must be Danny McCord, growed up.' When everyone looked at him, he cleared his throat and added quickly, 'Well, Danny'd know the Whetstones, the McCords chouse down mustangs for their remudas in here every season. Some of their own mavericks, too. Danny worked 'em plenty with Al.'

There were murmurings of agreement but Gill scoffed. 'Judas Priest! He was only a kid when he quit Arrerhead!'

'Mebbe,' Watty spoke up again, 'but Big Al had him under his wing before that and I know for a fact they spent a lot of time in these hills. He'd know 'em well.'

172

Others agreed with him and Barton Gill scowled. 'Well, don't much matter who he is, it don't help us! We're still stuck out here while he hides an' makes fools of us all.'

'Riders comin'!' called a man from the rear, who was sitting his horse close to the top of the rise where they were halted. 'Looks like they could be — yeah! It's a bunch from Arrerhead — recognize Dean's palomino.'

Gill was relieved although he didn't show it and when Dean McCord led his men in and reined up, he lifted a hand in casual greeting.

'Good to see you, Dean.' About as sincere as a snake-oil drummer closing in on a sale. 'Need some more men. We was just makin' a plan of action, but I guess you'll know the Whetstones better'n us, so, you want to take a look at this map with me?'

Dean ignored the map the sheriff proffered.

'Tear that up an' hang it in your privy, be more use to you. I'll leave a

173

man with you to guide you through,' Dean said, ignoring Gill's flush of annoyance. 'I'm taking my men to a couple places I know Danny had been with Big Al. We can arrange signals — smoke column broke into three, or gunshots — say two fast, pause, one more. Two more if it's urgent.'

Gill didn't like Dean taking over so quickly but the young rancher was making sense. He turned to an Arrowhead cowhand sitting a grulla mount on his left.

'Clete, you used to come up with Big Al huntin' mustangs. You stay with the sheriff and his men, take 'em to any part of the hills you figure Danny would know.'

'Sure, boss.'

The sheriff spoke quickly. 'You sayin' you figure Brett really *is* Danny, come back?'

'Well, it seems a good bet. OK, Clete. We'll see you back at the ranch. 'Luck, Bart!'

He signed to his men. They wheeled

174

their mounts and rode up and over the rise, heading straight into the shadowy hills, leaving the sheriff with his mouth hanging open.

'Where the hell's he think he's goin'?' Gill growled but Clete just shrugged.

'We'd best move, Sher'ff. Once them shadows start around noon we'll have a lot more trouble findin' tracks in this snake nest.'

Goddamnit! Everyone seemed set on taking over from him! Barton Gill growled to himself, but he lifted his reins and set his mount to following the grulla, the posse tagging along.

He was good and mad, but would have been a sight madder if he had known that when the posse was first sighted as Dean led his men towards the hills, the young rancher had said to Clete,

'That idiot Gill won't know where the hell to go. I'll leave you with him, Clete. You take him an' them townsmen in there and you lose 'em. Till sundown, at least.'

Clete had grinned. 'Be a pleasure, boss. I owe Gill for tossin' me in jail last payday. Missed out on a session with Tiny Tess.' He lifted his reins but held the grulla as it started to move. 'Dean, s'pose, just by some luck, we spot Brett?'

Dean gave him a hard, bleak look. 'Shoot on sight! And that applies to all of you. There'll be a bonus for the man who gets him. When we leave the Whetstones, we leave Brett dead, then it don't matter who he really is — was.'

Clete nodded and rode off. This was a chore he would do quite happily.

Meanwhile, Dean would take his men to a place he knew Danny had favoured, and which not many folk knew about, let alone how to get there.

An old Indian hideaway, called Gunbutt.

★ ★ ★

Danny's directions came to Brett more easily than he expected. Those last

176

days, Danny had been incoherent a lot of the time, slurring words, coughing, even giving an occasional derisive laugh.

He rolled his head from side to side on the sweat-soaked pillow, lifted his one hand, grabbing violently at Brett when he thought Danny was bad enough to call in the doctor.

'No! Damn it, Brett!' He had little breath to spare but the flare in that lonely eye held Brett anchored to his chair. 'Lemme get — it said . . . ' After a lot of gasping, head lolling loosely, he lifted up again and said his piece, even though most times now it took twice, three times as long as previously. Brett had to ask him to repeat many words.

'Jus' listen, dammit! Aw, hell! Gimme some paper. I still got one hand. I'll draw you a map.

Brett was dubious, but Danny managed it, although it was pretty crude. But he had always idly sketched outlines of things: horses, riders, guns,

177

knives, vegetation, and now, instead of laboriously trying to write directions on the map, he sketched rough scenes of what to look for.

It exhausted him — exhausted Brett, too, straining to hear or savvy what Danny was trying to tell him.

On the fifth day it seemed that Danny had said all he wanted to — or all he was able to. Looking pale and corpselike as Brett sat by the bed he opened that one eye and said,

'Just one more thing . . . '

'OK, Danny. I'm listening.'

Brett waited while the man's gaze bored into him as he prepared his last request.

'A — gun.'

Brett straightened, instantly alert. 'What?'

'With just — one bullet.'

'Aw, Jesus, Danny, no! I-I can't do that! Hell, man, I know things must look mighty bleak for you, but — '

'You — dunno — at — all. You owe — me — Brett. You promised me.

Anythin' I — wanted — you'd do it — or get it. *An' I want a — gun!'*

★ ★ ★

Resting their blowing mounts amongst huge sandstone boulders, cracked from winter ice and blizzards, Raina moved closer to Brett — an instinctive, involuntary movement.

He turned to look at her slowly, his face taut, eyes haunted-looking, as she twined her fingers in his and held tightly. She didn't ask if he had complied with Danny's wish; the answer was written plainly on his face.

'I think . . . probably . . . that it was for the best.' Her voice was barely above a whisper and brought no reply, nor reaction that she could see.

Neither of them knew how long they stayed that way — until Brett suddenly wrenched his hand free, stepped quickly forward behind a rock, signing for her to do the same.

'What is it?'

179

He pointed down to a winding trail a hundred feet below, straight down. Five horsemen were making their way slowly up the narrow trail, and the only place it led was to where they now stood.

Raina drew in a sharp breath, leaning on the rock as she watched. 'It's Dean McCord! And some of his hardcases! Though I don't see Rackman. He's the Arrowhead ramrod, a real trouble-maker, said to be a killer. I've had a lot of trouble with him pestering me. I'd expect him to be here.'

'Dean must've remembered Big Al brought Danny here when they were on mustang hunts.' Brett was already wiping his rifle's action with his oily cloth as he moved carefully around the big rock. 'Hold the horses. The gunfire's going to echo and slap around like a clap of thunder with all these rocks.'

'Don't shoot! I know the way down. We can be well on to the trail before they get up here.'

He paused, uncertain, instinct telling

him the best thing to do was to pick off as many of the riders as he could before they made cover — or detected his hiding place.

The decision was taken out of his hands.

A tall man in black cord trousers, black leather gunbelt and calfskin vest over a black shirt stepped out from behind a boulder, holding a sawn-off shotgun. His face was narrow and he was grinning, showing big, tobacco-stained teeth. He looked at them both with cold eyes as Raina breathed,

'Joel Rackman!'

'In person! Dean said to shoot you on sight, but seein' as he's so close I reckon he'd like a word or two with you, mister. Now drop that rifle, an' you, squaw, get back there agin the flat rock and keep your hands where I can see 'em.'

They obeyed. Rackman held the short shotgun in his left hand, pointed directly at the girl, thumb on one hammer spur. He took out his Colt

181

with his other hand and paused; if he triggered a signal to Dean, the shots could be heard by Gill and the posse that Clete was supposed to be losing in the maze of gulches and draws. The shots might give Gill a direction to find a way out and Dean sure wouldn't want them to turn up here before Brett was killed.

He decided he had better follow Dean's orders: shoot the man on sight. So he rammed the six-gun back into leather and started to change the shotgun over to his right hand again.

Brett, never one to miss a chance when a chance was all that stood between him and death, kicked a fist-sized stone lying against his boot. It didn't lift far off the ground but it thudded into Rackman's shin on his right leg.

He grunted involuntarily and the leg turned to rubber, throwing his body all aslant. Raina gasped as Brett hurled himself across the short space and rammed his head into Rackman's chest, hands groping for the shotgun. The ramrod had the hammer at half-cock and Brett's hand closed tightly over it, jamming any further movement.

Rackman was strong, hard-muscled from years of range work, and a man with much violence in him. He didn't struggle to fight Brett for the shotgun — he released it suddenly. Brett stumbled at the unexpected loss of resistance, and Rackman bared his teeth, chopped a blow down against the side of his jaw. Brett went down to one knee, the gun falling.

Rackman lifted a knee at his face, but Brett twisted away, rolled and came up on Rackman's left side. The big ramrod spun — and walked into a blow that took him in the middle of the face. Blood spurted and he stumbled. Brett quickly followed through with two lightning jabs, snapping Rackman's head back. He stepped to the rear to retain balance but Brett crowded him against the rock where Raina had been standing a few seconds before.

She circled the scuffling men carefully, her eye on the shotgun. Joel Rackman saw the direction of her gaze, took another blow in the temple and staggered, kicking at the gun.

It skidded across the ledge and sailed out into space, falling thirty feet on to another, wider ledge that merely jutted out from the slope, leading nowhere.

The gun fired.

The thunder of the single shot slapped and echoed through the Whetstones, giving the fighting men pause for a moment. Rackman grinned suddenly.

Brett knew why: it would bring Dean and his men running.

So he had to stop Rackman in his tracks. *Now!*

They had been circling each other while these thoughts flashed through their heads and, simultaneously, they closed, bodies jarring, fists hammering, heads butting, both men using elbows, boots and knees.

They staggered and floundered all

184

over the precarious ledge outside the cave. Raina was worried that they might step over the edge and follow the shotgun down.

Then Brett took a right hook in the midriff that jack-knifed him, gagging. Rackman, breathing heavily, blood running from crushed nostrils and split lips, stepped in and snapped up a knee towards Brett's contorted face. Raina hurled a rock she had been holding; it punched the ramrod between the shoulder blades. He staggered, and almost fell, trying to get his raised leg down again for balance.

It gave Brett the moment he needed to recover from the blow to the plexus. He couldn't yet breathe deeply but, coughing and fighting for air, he grabbed Rackman's ears and brought the man's face down towards *his* rising knee. It took the Arrowhead man on the forehead. Rackman's arms flailed as he was hurled back. His body slammed into the rock beside Raina, causing her to jump aside hurriedly. The back of his

185

head made a dull sound as it connected with the sandstone.

Rackman's legs buckled a little but Brett stepped in, arms blurred like full-speed pistons as he worked on the man's mid-section. When the ramrod started to sag, he drove his fists into the bloody face, ramming the man's head back against the rock again.

Joel Rackman's eyes rolled up, showing the whites, before his legs gave way and he toppled forward.

Brett, stumbling, reached for Raina's arm, dragged her towards him and sent her stumbling up the short path to where their horses were tethered. He snatched up his rifle and hat, wiped the back of a hand across his bleeding nostrils, smearing red.

He didn't have enough breath to speak, but trudged past the unconscious Rackman to where Raina already had the horses' reins in her hands.

'That shotgun blast'll bring Dean and his men.'

He shook his head, fumbling for his

186

mount's reins, sliding his rifle into the saddle scabbard.

'It — it went off — thirty feet — below,' he gasped. 'They'll make — for that ledge — mightn't even see this one.'

She looked dubious but it was certainly a possibility, depending on how clearly Dean and his crew had heard the blast.

They mounted. Brett sagged over the saddle at first, struggling to swing a leg across to the second stirrup. He waved the girl on impatiently and she started up a trail so narrow their legs brushed the boulders on either side. They hadn't gone more than a few yards before a six-gun triggered behind them. Instinctively, they ducked low over their mounts but no bullets cut air over their heads or ricocheted from the boulders. Raina frowned, catching Brett's eye.

'Rackman — signalling! He'll bring Dean up here! *Ride like hell!*'

They spurred their mounts, both animals complaining some, not liking the confining trail. Then bullets started whining off the rocks behind and above as Rackman reloaded and, having made his signal, kept firing after them. The shots would give Dean a definite direction now and the hunters would arrive quickly.

Just as well the Indian girl knew the area. She made a sharp turn, tight enough to require backing and filing a little to get the horses around, and then they were safe from Joel Rackman's bullets.

But they didn't know where Dean and his crew were. If they found the trail up to the cave ledge, they were bound to see the lower fork that would bring them out closer to where they were now riding.

Raina told Brett this, and when she pointed out where the trails crossed he squeezed past on his roan and dismounted, leaving the reins to trail. Crouching, he moved forward amongst some low rocks and she heard him swear.

'Are they in sight?'

He nodded, but had his rifle to his shoulder now, drawing a bead on the riders she could not see.

The Winchester crashed in a thundering volley of shots and ricocheting bullets, the din augmented by whinnying horses and cursing, shouting men. When she drew close enough to see, first leaning from the saddle to lift the roan's reins and have them ready for Brett's retreat, she saw the confusion below.

Horses were crashing into one another as the riders, trying to turn back, ran into those coming up from behind. She saw one man rise in the stirrups and tumble sideways, to be trampled under the stomping feet of the frightened horses. Another jumped from the saddle, misjudged and crashed into a high-standing rock, sliding down semi-conscious with blood on his face and one arm hanging limply.

She glimpsed Dean's red face as he shouted orders or curses or both, getting his six-gun out and shooting uptrail wildly. One of Brett's slugs ricocheted from sandstone beside him, stinging his face with erupting grit. He howled in rage but was jammed against the rock by one of his men forcing his way past in full retreat.

Suddenly, the log jam cleared and the Arrowhead men were spurring back down the trail. Brett had emptied his rifle by this time; he sat back and reloaded quickly, only thumbing in five shells before he started raking the trail with deadly fire once more.

Stumbling a little, he ran for his roan, hitting the stirrup fast and grabbing the reins from the girl.

'Come on!' he yelled. She was startled to see him wheeling his mount, spurring down the narrow trail *towards* Dean's crew as they still tried to settle their frightened mounts and calm the wounded men, who were just as scared as the animals.

Raina's heart was in her mouth as she spurred after Brett, it was a very dangerous move. But Brett rode into the bunched men full tilt, swinging his smoking rifle, the barrel cracking against heads, toppling riders from their saddles.

One of the men he hit was Dean McCord. The barrel took him across the head, foresight ripping flesh. Even as the Arrowhead owner clawed at his face, he was falling. Raina instinctively swerved aside to miss him but wished in a flash that she had ridden him down.

Hands clawed at her. She lashed out with her quirt, feeling the short, plaited rawhide biting into flesh. Their mounts were plunging, rolling their eyes, but answered the urging of the spurs and the tugs on the reins.

In a matter of seconds — violent, dangerous seconds — they were through and thundering down the trail with no one in front of them.

Her heart hammered against her ribs as she rode up alongside Brett. He had blood smeared across his rugged features. 'You are a madman!' she told him. But she grinned when she said it.

11

No Mercy

Clete Mitchell heard the shooting and, swearing under his breath, saw that Barton Gill and most of the posse had heard too.

'Where the hell did that come from?' snapped Gill, angry because of the way they had been riding through a maze of gulches and draws, getting nowhere. Although he had never been in the Whetstones before, the sheriff instinctively knew that they were being given the runaround. 'Anyone tell?'

The rest of the posse looked worried, shaking heads.

'I think we're damn well lost!' Gill snapped, glaring at Clete. 'Worse than we were before you showed up! Seems to me you could be losin' us on purpose, Clete!'

Bradley, the oldster, concurred, as did a couple of others. The big storeman, Watty, spat tobacco juice and decided to speak up. 'I seen that needle rock from three different angles so far, and we ain't no closer. The hell you playin' at, Clete?'

Mitchell, a hard man, spread his hands, face sober.

'I don't 'play' when Dean McCord gives me an order. He said to lead you men into the Whetstones, an' try to find any tracks left by Brett.'

'You ain't done a helluva lot of good so far!'

'That's 'cause there *ain't* any tracks. None that I can see, anyways. Hell, you fellers are s'posed to be keepin' your eyes open, too! You spot somethin', say so, and we'll take a closer look.'

The sheriff seemed thoughtful and suddenly palmed up his six-gun. Clete Mitchell stiffened. 'Hey!'

'Take us back to where we met McCord.'

'What? We been ridin' for hours. You

193

wanna waste all that time?'

'You son of a bitch, we *have* wasted all that time!' He cocked the pistol and colour drained from Clete's horse-face. The man lifted one hand from his saddle horn.

'All right! Judas! We have to scout around, not knowin' which way Brett might've come? What the hell you blamin' me for? I cain't find tracks where there ain't any.'

For a moment he thought Gill was going to shoot anyway, then they heard more distant gunfire and the sheriff's face hardened.

'You take us out of here, or I'll put a bullet through your gunhand. Then your goddamn feet!'

Clete wasn't feeling so tough and cocky now. He licked his lips. 'OK, OK! Hell's teeth, a man tries to help — '

He ducked and yelled as Barton Gill put a shot over his head. 'Get ridin', you bastard, or I'll cripple you and leave you here!'

Under the hostile gazes of the rest of

the posse, Clete muttered something to himself and turned his mount. As he passed the sheriff, Gill halted him.

'Take his guns,' he ordered and two men crowded the protesting Clete until he handed over his Colt and rifle.

'I hope we don't run into Brett!' he said.

'Not much chance of that,' Gill snapped. 'I think Dean wants the sonuver for himself and your job was to deliberately keep us lost. But I'll take that up with Dean when I see him. Now let's go!'

⋆ ⋆ ⋆

The Arrowhead men were a sorry sight after Brett and Raina had burst through them. Three were wounded, one seriously, and Dean, looking as battered as any of them, angrily sent all three wounded back to the ranch.

'Send out three men to replace you,' Dean snapped. 'No, wait. We've got a crew clearing the western slope near the dam — they're closer. Who we got out there, Joel?'

The battered ramrod spat some more blood from his busted mouth and thought for a moment. 'Five men, but them Mallin brothers're only kids. They wouldn't be much good to us in a shoot-out.'

'Then, for Chris'sakes, tell me who *would* be some good to us!'

Rackman gave him a hard look out of his left eye, the one that wasn't blackened and swollen. 'There's Buster Snell, Mike Trail, and Boone. They're all pretty tough, an' won't mind going' on fightin' wages.' There was a slyness to his words and Dean glared, nodded slowly.

'Thanks for reminding me about fighting wages, Joel!' Dean gritted. '*Just* what I need! All right. Jingo, you ride on ahead and tell Buster and the other two to meet us at that big pine above the dam. Tell the Mallins I want all the stumps cleared pronto. The herds we're holding in the south pasture are mighty

196

restless: too crowded. We need somewhere to send at least half of 'em. They can work some overtime if they want.'

The young ranny chosen for the chore quickly dragged his horse around and spurred away. Dean watched him for a few moments, then swung slightly left so he could see the wounded trio on their way back to Arrowhead.

'I think when we sight Brett, we drive him back this way.' Dean rubbed gently at his bruised and cut face, dried blood flaking off.

Rackman frowned. 'On to Arrowhead?'

'Why the hell not? Gill's got no jurisdiction here. He don't even need to know we've got Brett. Then we can work on that son of a bitch a little and find out just who he is, what he's doing here, and how much he knows.'

'Knows what, boss?' asked one of the bruised and battered men innocently. But he wilted under McCord's stare.

'*You* don't need to know!'

⋆　⋆　⋆

'Is that a lake over there?' Brett pointed through the trees to where water glinted.

Raina shook her head. 'Arrowhead's dam. Largest in the county, if not the territory.'

Brett frowned. 'Danny doesn't show it on his map.'

'No, he'd left long before they put it in. It was after the '79 floods. The heavy rains partly filled a big catchment area on Arrowhead. Big Al called in an engineer to see if they could divert the river that way and build a dam. Now Arrowhead will never run short of water.'

'What about the spreads downstream? Does Arrowhead control their water from his dam?'

'Ye-es. But Al bought them all — not without some claims of underhand dealing, and a lot of bad blood, but he won out, so the water's really feeding all McCord land.'

'Arrowhead's mighty big, then; the dam must be, too.'

'Yes, huge. It's one of Arrowhead's biggest assets.'

'Let's ride over that way.'

She looked at him in surprise. 'That'll take us on to Arrowhead land!'

He smiled with his swollen lips, moving them just a little. 'And the last place they'll expect to find us.'

'I withdraw my earlier remark, Brett. You're not just mad, you're absolutely crazy!'

★ ★ ★

Dean and his men had gathered by the tall pine on the high ground that overlooked the dam. The water spread like a huge metal sheet under the hammering sunlight, covering several acres. The three hardcases from the pasture had arrived, eager for some fighting wages and the change from the backbreaking work of felling trees and either dragging the trunks away after

199

branch-stripping, or reducing them to manageable size in the big sawpit. It was filthy, exhausting work.

Rackman was in a foul mood, stiff and sore from his fight with Brett. The other two men who had been gun-whipped were wishing Dean had sent them back with the three who had the worst injuries.

Dean McCord was confident now that he was going to wrap up the whole thing on this day. His face was throbbing and he hated the constant taste of blood from where his teeth had cut the inside of his cheek, but he pushed all those things to the back of his mind as he looked around at his group.

These were some of the toughest men employed by Arrowhead. If they could herd Brett and that damn squaw woman on to Arrowhead land . . .

'Goddlemighty, Dean, *look*!'

Frowning, annoyed that his thoughts had been interrupted, Dean looked up sharply at the sound of Buster Snell's voice.

Snell was a blocky man, shoulders so wide that he had to turn side on to get through some doorways. He had a jet-black beard, which he stroked agitatedly when he was excited. Right now his left hand was running up and down the dark strands while he pointed downhill through the timber with his right.

There were two riders down there, close to the dam's huge headgates, oblivious to the men on the high slope.

'Brett and the Injun gal!' Rackman said unnecessarily, standing in his stirrups. 'By hell, Dean! This is a piece of luck!'

McCord acknowledged that with a slow, satisfied nod. For a moment he almost smiled. 'Go down quietly and stay inside the tree line, but spread out in a half-moon once in position. When I signal, close in. Only place they'll have to go is in the dam.' This time he did smile, widely. 'A couple of million gallons of water, thirty feet deep. Boys, I think we might have us a leetle ol' party at Arrowhead tonight!'

That brought grins all round, but Boone, ugly as sin and almost as dirty, had to spoil it.

'Could be bonus time, eh, boss?'

Dean's smile disappeared like someone blowing out a candle flame. 'More like don't-get-smart-with-the-boss time. Unless you want to find out just how deep that dam water is.'

Everyone was very still, very silent. They knew Dean's quick-changing moods and had seen men suffer because of them.

But the sight of Brett and Raina sitting their mounts, unsuspecting, made Dean's trigger finger itch and the feeling of triumph overwhelmed his bad temper.

'Let's go down an' get 'em. Might be we'll have a little party with that damn squaw, right here, before we go back to headquarters — if you boys ain't too squeamish.'

They indicated by several ribald remarks that they could overcome any problems in that area and enjoy whatever Raina Redbird had to offer.

''Offer' be damned!' Joel Rackman said, rubbing his bruised and cut face. 'We take what we want.'

Dean nodded. 'Yeah. This time, no mercy!'

★ ★ ★

Brett and Raina were just as surprised when the men came galloping out of the timber as those same men had been when they spotted the fugitives at the edge of the dam.

Brett had dismounted and was standing on the very edge of the bank, as close as he could get to the back-slanting, log-and-concrete wall, with the biggest set of headgates he had ever seen on any dam.

In fact, this was the largest private dam he had ever seen — and he had travelled a lot of miles over the years.

'You could stand a troop of cavalry, mounts, caissons and all, on those gates

203

if they were laid flat,' he allowed.

Raina nodded, seeing the spurting water where the gates didn't quite meet in the middle — or where the immense pressure of the water behind was holding them from a flush fit, pushing relentlessly.

'It must have cost a small fortune,' she opined. 'I remember the county wanted to buy in but Big Al wouldn't hear of it; he wanted total control over the water supply at this end of the basin.'

Brett turned to look at a small notched-log hut just within a line of young trees on the bank above the fallaway where water trickled and formed a small stream far below.

The hut housed the rack-and-pinion gears for opening and closing the gates; the long shafts required were invisible from here, extending out to the gates under water. He started to move a little closer, then saw the bunch of men surging out of the timber, sweeping in in a wide arc.

'Raina! Get out of here!' he shouted, drawing his Colt even as she turned quickly, spotted the riders and spurred away. She had been holding the reins of Brett's mount and dragged the animal with her, tossing him the reins even as he started shooting. He caught the reins as she veered away and dodged to his left, the horse coming willingly enough. One of Dean's riders, Boone, reeled in the saddle, slid to one side, hanging on desperately.

As Brett swung aboard his mount, bullets whistling over his head, he fired again, rammed the six-gun back into the holster and slid the Winchester out of the scabbard, using his knees to spin the horse, and send it racing along the edge of the dam.

He got off one shot and the young ranny called Jingo toppled from the saddle. The lever worked as Dean's voice reached him:

'That'll be enough!'

Brett snapped his head around; he saw that Rackman and Dean had closed in on Raina, had her under their guns. She looked around wildly but had nowhere to go and had to rein up.

'We couldn't miss at this range!' Dean called and Brett slid the rifle back into the scabbard as he halted the mount and lifted his hands shoulder high.

Joel Rackman rode in and took Brett's Colt, rapping the barrel across his head hard enough to knock off his hat. Brett sagged in the saddle, a little blood trickling from beneath his hairline, but he held on to the horn, his skull feeling like it had been shattered.

Rackman bared his teeth as the others rode up, the two wounded men, pale and bleeding. He put his mount alongside Raina's. She looked at him apprehensively.

'Well, finally got you where I want you, huh, squaw lady! You make a good-lookin' Injun in them buckskins.' Rackman gloated, watching Brett fighting to stay conscious. 'Let's see how you look without 'em . . . '

12

Square-away Time

'That shootin's comin' from Arrowhead!' said Sheriff Barton Gill, reining down on the slope that led to a grassy bench above the river.

Clete Mitchell spurred upslope, lashing his mount, reined down as soon as he topped out. 'Hey! There's a whole bunch of riders down at the dam!' He fought his sweating mount, sawing with the bit. 'Judas! They've got Brett! And the Injun woman!'

Gill was already riding up to join Clete, now he used his mount to muscle the man back behind the brush.

'You skylined, you idiot!'

'Hell, it don't matter if they see us. I work here.'

Gill didn't answer; he leaned forward, straining to see. 'That goddamn

Brett! What the hell's he doin' up this way? Mebbe aimin' to blow the dam?'

'Jesus! He wouldn't do that, would he? It'd drown this whole end of the basin!'

'It's Arrowhead's basin.'

Clete pursed his lips. 'Well, I guess we dunno how mean the sonuver can get, but don't matter now. Dean's got him. Oh-oh!' He stood in his stirrups and Gill frowned, straining to see past the man's mount. 'Hey! They're startin' to strip off the squaw's clothes!'

'Come on!' Gill said, tight-lipped, drawing his gun. 'Time Dean realized the law applies to the McCords, same as everyone else.'

'Aw, she's only an Injun, Bart.'

'I don't care about her, don't even like her. But I like Dean and that Rackman even less.' Gill triggered three fast shots into the air, startling the rest of the posse still below on the slope — and sure getting the attention of the laughing men circling Raina on horseback. They reached out as they rode, trying to pull her buckskin shirt down over her shoulders. ''Fact, I don't like you much, either, Clete. Let's get down there.'

Brett was under Dean's gun and his hands seemed to be tied to the saddle horn, or they were making him hold on to it so they could be sure where his hands were. He snapped his head up and around as Gill's shots crashed and echoed; for once he was glad to see the lawman and his posse.

'Just hold it right there!' Gill bawled, smoking pistol still in hand as he rode up.

Rackman and the others pulled back from the girl who seemed more angry than afraid. She shrugged her torn buckskin shirt back over her bare shoulder which bore red scratches from someone's horny nails. Her eyes were blazing as she rammed her horse into Rackman's and, as he fought the reins, she ripped her fingernails down both sides of his face. He roared in pain and tossed his head wildly, almost fell from the staggering mount. Her breast heaved as she glared at Dean McCord and prepared to run her mount at him. Dean calmly lifted his Colt.

'My bullet'll get to you quicker than that idiot sheriff!' he warned.

She reined aside and rode up next to Brett. Rackman was cursing foully, snarling now as he looked around for the girl. Brett, who had been gripping the saddle horn tightly at Dean's orders, but was not bound, jammed home his spurs and his horse leapt away like an arrow, whinnying. It cut between Rackman's mount and Raina. The animals went down, whickering and kicking, as the riders threw themselves out of the saddles. Rolling in the dust they both started up, ready to tear each other apart, but a gun thundered and a bullet ploughed the ground between them. They froze, looked up as Barton Gill rode in, his smoking pistol menacing them.

'Stay put!' He glared, shifted his angry gaze to Dean McCord. 'Your plan to get my posse lost didn't work!'

Dean arched his eyebrows. 'What the hell're you talking about?'

'Ah, forget it! I'm here now and I aim to take my prisoner back to town. Make that prisoners. She helped him escape.'

'Can you prove that, Sheriff?' asked Brett coldly.

'Reckon so. Either way, she's been helping you on the run and that's good enough. Shuck your gun.'

'Rackman's already taken it,' Brett said, looking at the bloody streaks with pieces of flesh dangling on the ramrod's savage face. They must be stingingly painful, those deep scratches. The man scowled, wrenched off his neckerchief and dabbed at his mauled, bleeding face.

'You're trespassin', Bart,' Dean said suddenly. 'You're on private land here — without permission.'

'That so? Well, last time I looked, Arrowhead was still in my county and as I'm sheriff I don't need your *permission* to pursue a fugitive anywhere I damn please! You want, I can quote you part of my commission, goes somethin' like this: 'A duly elected lawman in pursuit of his duty is hereby authorized to cross all boundaries, Territorial, State, Federal or *Private, without let or hindrance* by any person, and, further, if that person shall attempt to delay, halt or otherwise restrain said lawman — ''

'All right, all right! Damn you, Bart! This is a private deal and you know it. You OK'd more than one when Big Al was alive.' He lowered his voice to a more reasonable level. 'I'll return Brett to you after I finish with him.'

'You'll return him to me right now, or you'll see what the inside of my jail looks like from the wrong side of the bars.'

Brett smiled secretly to himself; this was more a contest of mental strength than of who was in the right. Each of the men glared hotly at the other, intent on imposing his will.

'You better listen, Bart! I've taken

212

over from Big Al. You did what he told you!'

Gill flushed. 'If it suited me.'

'Dammit! He saw you right!'

Gill's eyes narrowed. 'Which you're yet to do.'

Dean frowned slightly, then smiled crookedly. 'Ah! That's where we're at! OK, that'll be attended to, you have my word. Now we understand each other?'

'Reckon so. But I need to take my prisoners with me.' Gill's jaw jutted, lending his stubbornness more strength.

Under his breath, Dean cursed the man for the fool he really was, but tried to keep his voice level and reasonable. 'Take the squaw, if you want, but I need to talk with Brett. There're things I must know about him.' He even managed a faint smile. 'Leave him with me overnight. Clete and Joel can deliver him to you in the morning.' He flicked his gaze to Brett's unreadable face. 'I'll be through with him by then.'

Bart Gill appeared to consider the suggestion. 'You and me better have a

213

private talk first, before I can agree to that or any other kinda . . . arrangement.'

Dean hoped he managed to cover the exasperated look that he knew wanted to twist his face. But he was too close to finding out how much Brett knew and what was his real motivation for harassing Arrowhead, so he nodded slowly.

'All right. We'll go to the ranch house, have a talk over some supper, followed by bourbon that's just arrived from Kentucky. Revenue seals not even broken yet.'

Anyone could see that that appealed to Barton Gill — and likely most of the men within hearing, but only the sheriff had an invitation.

'You men wait here — and tie up Brett — the damn gal too, she gives any trouble.'

Big Watty spoke up as the posse men moved restlessly.

'Sheriff, we been rode into the damn ground all day an' we ain't even ate decent yet!'

214

'You can eat when we get back to town.'

'Not while you're fillin' your belly and settlin' what you eat with bonded bourbon!' growled Watty and he was backed up by the rest of the posse.

Dean was impatient and snapped, 'We're wasting time! Bring your men in and they can eat with the crew. We'll lock up Brett and the squaw.'

Gill, as usual not liking anyone making decisions for him, nodded grudgingly. 'OK, I'll go along with that.'

Then they all started at the sound of a distant explosion. Dean looked sharply at Rackman, who shrugged.

'That'll be the Mallins. You said you wanted that pasture cleared, pronto, and with only the two of 'em left to work it, I guess they decided to blast out the biggest stumps.'

'Well someone ride out and tell the fools to quit using dynamite. Christ! That herd we've got jammed into the east pasture's already spooky. Ah, tell 'em when they come in for supper to bring the dynamite with 'em; they can get an early start come daybreak. Rest of you bring Brett and the gal and let's get going. I want this thing finished today! Come on! Move, damnit!'

* * *

While Barton Gill ate with deep concentration, enjoying his roast duck and garden vegetables, Belle appeared in the doorway of the big ranch kitchen and motioned Dean to join her.

He looked at her puzzledly as she closed the door leading to the dining room. He saw by her heightened colour and tight lips that she was upset about something.

'What happened to Joel's face?'

He blinked. 'Ah, Rackman and Clete were havin' a bit of fun, riding round the squaw, seeing who could pull her buckskin shirt down to her waist first.' He jerked a thumb towards the dining room on the other side of the wall. 'Gill arrived and broke it up. Raina near tore

216

Rackman's eyes out.'

'I told you long ago she shouldn't be allowed to run a business in town! One that pays pretty damn well, too!'

Not sure what one thing had to do with the other, her brother scratched his nose and said, 'Well, Joel Rackman's been trying to get into her bed for ages, everyone knows that. Guess he thought he had it made, till Gill showed up.' He stopped right there, remembering that once he had seen Rackman sneaking out of Belle's bedroom just before sunup. Ah, the old green-eyed monster had suddenly appeared!

'Bart's got her locked up in the toolshed, told me to take her supper. Me! Wait on a squaw? Like hell! I sent that kid you got working the stables. Why's Bart got her prisoner?'

'He reckons she smuggled Brett a derringer that got him outta jail, and has been leading him around the Whetstones ever since, dodging the posses.'

217

'Dammit! Then she's in it with him. We've got to finish this, Dean! I have a bad feeling about this Brett, I've said so all along. I don't believe he's Danny come back, but he knows too damn much. You see they kill him and kill that Indian bitch, too!'

'With Barton Gill within arm's reach? Talk sense, sis!'

She was shaking her head slowly. 'No wonder Pa used to despair over you sometimes! Use your head, *brother*! The tool shed's not a proper jail. The squaw can escape — and she'll be sure to try to get Brett out . . . ' She spread her hands. 'Desperate prisoners, *shot while trying to escape*!'

Dean frowned, and parted his lips, mulling it over. 'Could be done, I guess. Right!' He started towards the door so fast her mouth gaped slightly. 'I'd better pour another glass or so of that good bourbon into our knot-headed sheriff. When he wakes up in the morning, he'll still have his prisoners. Only thing is, they'll need burying!'

218

★　★　★

The rest of Dean's supper with the sheriff, who was well on the way to being drunk, being unable to resist the mellow top-grade bourbon, was interrupted by Clete Mitchell.

'Christ! I'll be out when I finish my meal! Whatever it is, Clete, it'll keep.'

'No, it won't, boss.' Clete was leery of giving Dean an argument — anyone could see he was mighty edgy, had been all day, and was fast losing patience. But Mitchell swallowed as the bleak gaze raked him. 'Link Mallin, the youngest one — He's hurt. Losin' a lotta blood.'

Dean glared, sighed, set down the whiskey bottle. Gill took the opportunity to pick it up and refill his glass.

'What happened?'

'That last charge of dynamite — fuse was too short. Link got a splinter through his side. Big one.'

Dean waved impatiently. 'Go see Belle. Wait. They bring in the dynamite?'

219

'Guess so. They had a pack-mule with 'em.'

'OK, OK. Now go find Belle. She can tend to him.'

★ ★ ★

He was refilling the sheriff's glass yet again when Belle McCord came hurrying in to where they were sitting in overstuffed chairs in the parlour, dinner over, smoking cigars. Gill looked sleepy, his face owlish.

Dean noted all the blood on his sister's apron and her sweat-beaded face.

'The splinter's too big and in too deep. It'll have to be cut out. I can't stop the bleeding so I've sent Link into town in the buckboard. His brother's gone with him and I told the wrangler to go, too. He has to pick up those two new horses that were reshod, anyway.'

'Good ol' sis.' Dean smirked; he liked that new bourbon, too, though he was nowhere near as drunk as the sodden

220

lawman. 'Always an eye to savin' a dollar.'

'I'm trying to save Arrowhead!' she snapped, weariness in her voice, as she wiped her hands on her apron. 'I'm going to wash up.' She flicked her gaze to Gill, who was already dozing in his chair. Belle lowered her voice. 'The kid's been told what to do at the toolshed when he collects the squaw's dishes. Might be a good time for you to have a 'talk' with Brett.'

Dean frowned. 'He'll be set up soon, and that'll be that. I've got to get double nighthawks on the herd, it's spooky as all hell. 'Fact, might send out the whole damn crew; they won't see nothin' they shouldn't round here then.'

She gripped his arm and he winced at the intensity of her clamping fingers. She stared up into his face. 'Dean, *interrogate* Brett before you kill him! We *have* to know who sent him, just what he knows, what he aims to do! *Then* you can arrange for him to be

221

shot while escaping — and don't forget *that damn Injun girl!*' She shook him. 'Damn you, Dean! Clear your head! All of Arrowhead's at stake here. Not to mention our lives!'

Her blazing words and anger got through to Dean, clearing away the mild alcoholic haze that had been slowly settling him into a state of relaxation.

He pushed her hand off his arm, angry. 'All right! Don't be so damn bossy! You're sure Big Al's daughter!'

'And you're supposed to be his son! Start acting like it.'

She turned and hurried towards her room. Dean, scowling, looked at the now snoring Gill, shook himself, then strode towards the door, going out into the night.

Some men were still sitting around the long table outside the bunkhouse, a few smoking, a couple still eating. One of these was Clete Mitchell, while Joel Rackman, his raw face gleaming with salve, smoked broodily, alone, leaning a shoulder against an awning post. He swivelled his eyes towards his boss.

'Get Clete.'

'He ain't finished supper yet.'

Dean's eyes almost popped out of his head. 'I don't care if he's in the middle of sparkin' Big Mouth Bertha in Dolly Dibbles' Den — get Clete! And come down to the root cellar! We're gonna have a talk with Brett!'

Rackman was sure glad that wasn't *his* name tonight.

13

Broken Arrow

Raina sat in the dark discomfort of the toolshed, feeling the fat-heavy meal she had eaten sitting soggily in her stomach. She hadn't been in the least hungry but it had been bred into her long ago that when there was food, eat; it could be a long time before the next meal.

An old Indian dictum, hard to shake.

She was rubbing her teeth with a water-moistened finger to rid them of the coating of residual fat when she suddenly paused. *The door hadn't sounded the same when that stable boy left with the empty dishes!*

She hadn't heard the click of the lock, just the door closing against the frame. It was totally dark in here although a few lights could be seen

224

between the warped vertical planks of the walls. The roof sloped towards the back and, being tall, she had to stoop as she groped her way to the front; they had been careful not to leave any tools she could use as a weapon or for breaking out.

The door opened outwards under her touch. Cool night air rushed in. She could see the outline of the bunkhouse and beyond, and lower on the slope, the main house itself. Big Al had built close to the creek, before he could afford the luxury of a kitchen pump, to save his wife carrying pails of water any further than necessary.

There were lights in the big house, still one or two in the bunkhouse, another in the cookhouse. She had heard Dean crankily dispatching night-hawks earlier, worried about his herds. He seemed to think they had been spooked by the Mallin brothers using dynamite to blast tree stumps this afternoon and, as overcrowding had already made them jittery, he ordered almost all the crew to nighthawk duty. It seemed like an overreaction to her; not that she knew much about ranching. But, a few minutes ago, she had heard Dean bawling for Rackman and Clete, and then yells and crashes from the root cellar where they had imprisoned Brett.

She suddenly knew why Dean had sent so many men out to the distant pasture, beyond those hogback rises, out of sight of the main house: *he didn't want witnesses!*

For 'what' she didn't dare think about, but now that she was outside the shed: *Wait!* It had been too easy! That kid hadn't made any attempt to turn the key in the lock, had even left the tongue pushed in so the door *couldn't* lock.

So, she was meant to escape — or was she only meant to try to escape, and be *shot!*

The Indian in her, always suspicious of the devious ways of the white man, made her step back just inside the shed.

226

There would be someone waiting out there in the darkness — waiting for her.

They wouldn't shoot her too close to the ranch buildings, they would want it to look like she really *had* been escaping. No doubt she would be found with some rusty old tool that could be used as a weapon lying near her hand. And there would be scars in the wood around the door lock. Barton Gill would read the signs: she broke out and was running away when she was challenged by the guard, shot when she tried to attack him with whatever tool they left with her.

There was still noise coming from the root cellar; she could see the glow of a lamp outlining the entrance, just below ground level. Curses. The crash of shelves or their contents. Someone yelled '*Watch out!*' She smiled slowly, Brett seemed to be showing some resistance.

She stooped and groped about, looking for a good-sized rock, and a man's voice said, to her left, and slightly behind her,

227

'You won't find nothin' to help you, squaw! Just straighten slow and we'll take us a leetle walk over the rise an' . . . see what happens, eh?'

There were no rocks that she could feel. But there was gravel. She straightened slowly, gripping a handful, squinted, and saw his silhouette against the stars. He had his hand on his gun butt but the weapon was still in its holster. She whipped the gravel into his face, hard, the stones stinging, one hitting him in the eye and bringing a cry of pain from him. She was on him while he was off balance, grabbed his shirtfront and flung him down the slope against the hardwood shed. The breath gusted from him and before he could regain it, she brought up a knee into his crotch, seized his ears and smashed his head into the shed, three times, with savage force.

Before he crumpled completely, she was unbuckling the gunbelt.

At the same time, she heard Dean's angry, muffled shout from the root cellar.

'By God, you'll tell us who you are and who sent you *right now*, or I'll cut your damn ears off!'

They had come for Brett immediately the sloping door of the root cellar had been thrown back.

They hadn't sent him any food — an indication that he wouldn't be *needing* any — and he had eventually found a jar of preserved pears and opened the waxed-over cork stopper. His fingers and chin were sticky with syrup but the fruit tasted marvellous.

When the door was flung open and Rackman and Clete Mitchell crowded down the narrow aisle, Dean holding a lantern, Brett turned and hurled the half-empty jar of pears. It missed Rackman by an inch but Clete wasn't quite fast enough to get his hands up. It thudded into his forehead, knocking off his hat, splashing sticky syrup in his face. Cursing, he clawed at his eyes, and Rackman straight-armed Brett back against a row of shelves. Bottles of preserves were shaken loose, glass

229

broke, crunched under his boots.

'Hold him, goddammit!' yelled Dean.

Rackman cornered Brett, swung a punch into the prisoner's chest. Brett grunted, ducked the next blow, rose swiftly inside the swing and brought the top of his head up under the ramrod's jaw. The man staggered back, tangling with the still floundering Mitchell, while Dean hopped about, trying to get a clear view of what was happening.

Rackman was dazed and Brett drove his raw, bleeding face into the end of a row of shelves. Dean saw his chance, stepped over Rackman's sprawling form and slammed his six-gun across the side of Brett's head. The prisoner stumbled heavily into the earthen wall and Dean kicked his legs out from under him.

As he sprawled, Dean kicked him again, grabbed Clete and flung him towards Brett. 'Hold the bastard! *Hold him!*'

Clete grabbed Brett's arm and heaved him upright. Rackman, bleeding, dazed, but fighting mad, grabbed his other arm, drove the top of his head into Brett's face. He fell back, then Dean was standing in front of the sagging man.

He had holstered his Colt, set his boots wide and firm, then hammered Brett's midriff, chest and face. His arms blurred, shoulders twisting and working, putting a lot of force behind each blow. Brett's legs began to buckle and Dean, breath hissing through nostrils and open mouth, stepped back, reached out to twist his fingers in Brett's sweaty hair, lifted his bloody face.

'Now. *Who the hell are you?*'

Brett opened his eyes slowly, just a little, gathered a mouthful of bloody spittle and spat it into Dean's face.

The rancher roared in his fury and stepped in, knee jerking into Brett's belly, elbow smashing into his jaw, knuckles bouncing off his head, until Dean realized he was hurting his own hands and stopped.

'Don't let him fall!' he yelled as his men made to release their grips. He fumbled in his pocket and brought out a jack-knife. His hands shook as he opened the blade. It caught the light from the lantern, bounced it around the low, shored-up roof, like a fluttering white butterfly. He grabbed Brett's jaw with an iron grip, the fingers of his left hand whitening with pressure. With the other hand, he held the knife-blade inches in front of Brett's eyes.

'Now! Tell me who you are and who sent you, or I'll cut your damn ears off!' He twisted his mouth into a crooked grin. 'Blade's not too sharp, so I'll have to do a little sawing. You tell me if it gets to be too much and holler 'Nuff!'' OK? That's all I'm saying. It's your turn now. You got about five seconds to start talkin'!'

Brett eyed that blade; he did not like knives when they became weapons. As a tool, that was fine, but in the hands of some sadistic son of a bitch like Dean McCord . . .

Rackman and Clete changed their grips as he started to struggle and he

232

kicked out, his boot raking Dean's shin. The man howled involuntarily, stumbled back, bending in the middle, reaching for his burning, throbbing leg. The blade slashed, ripped through the front of Brett's blood-spotted shirt, the tip just raking his flesh.

The two Arrowhead hands tightened their grip, tried to throw him back against the wall, but weren't prepared for his sudden resistance. Their fingers slipped on his sweaty flesh and wet shirtsleeves — not much, but enough to enable Brett to jerk his arms free. He stumbled and had to fight for balance, cannoning into Dean, who was still trying to straighten up — and who still had the knife in his hand . . .

'Brett!'

He snapped his head up at the sound of Raina's voice, saw her standing in the slanted entrances. She tossed something in his direction: a six-gun.

He lunged over Dean, pushing the man's bent head down with one hand, snatched the spinning Colt out of the air with the other and smashed the lantern with the barrel. Hot oil splashed and flared, some finding the struggling Clete Mitchell. The man yelled and thrashed crazily, slapping at his blazing shirtsleeve and shoulder, crashing into shelves as he stormed towards the entrance.

He made a fine target and Brett triggered twice, his bullets driving Clete to his knees at the foot of the short steps. Rackman brought his gun around, but was too close to fire it. Instead of triggering, he tried to knock Brett off his feet with a short blow. The prisoner felt the gun clip his shoulder; it threw him sideways so that Dean McCord's shot missed, the bullet burning across Rackman's thigh. The ramrod yelled and cussed, but he should have been concentrating on Brett.

When he spun, looking for him in the flickering light from Clete's still burning clothes, he stared into the Colt's muzzle. He shook his head frantically, starting to lift his hands quickly. From Brett's crouched position it looked like Rackman was lifting his gun for a shot and he triggered.

Joel Rackman hurtled back, shuddering as the lead drove in, upwards, beneath the arch of his ribs. He was dead before he hit the ground.

And Brett was on the move, seeing Dean's back as the man knocked Raina off her feet and plunged out of the root cellar. He twisted, fired back into the cellar, snatched at Raina. But, even though dazed, she slapped at him with the bullet belt she had taken from the guard on the toolshed. The cartridge-weighted belt caught Dean across the side of his head and he sprawled sideways. Brett fired again and Dean jerked as lead took him high in one leg. Raina had tripped and was getting to her feet when Brett came charging out. His boot slipped on the bottom step and he sprawled as Dean fired wildly. The lead thunked into the doorframe and Brett's gun went off, his thumb releasing the hammer involuntarily.

Brett didn't see where the shot went but Dean fired again, so he figured he hadn't hit the man — and now his Colt was empty.

At the same time the posse men, who had been left in the bunkhouse after the ranch hands had been sent out on nighthawk duty, started yelling, demanding to know what the hell was happening.

And a bleary-eyed Barton Gill staggered out on to the porch, groping for his gun, calling in a slurred voice,

'Dean? You want some he'p?'

Raina was on her feet, steady now, and as Brett grabbed her arm and hauled her out of the sunken entrance to the root cellar, she thrust the cartridge belt and holster at him.

'Brett's escaping!' Dean roared.

The words sobered Gill even as Belle ran out on to the porch, shotgun in hand. 'Your posse!' she snapped at the befuddled lawman, who shook himself and nodded. 'Get them!'

'Posse wages just started again!' Gill

236

bawled. 'Grab your mounts! Don't let 'em get away!'

Belle saw shadows moving across behind the rise the cellar had been dug into, lifted the long-barrelled shotgun and fired. She stumbled with the recoil and the buckshot swirled harmlessly, well short of the running fugitives.

'Dean!' she called frantically. 'Where's Dean?'

'I'm ... here,' her brother called back, watching Gill trying to organize his few posse men. 'I'm shot ... '

Belle dropped the shotgun and ran towards the cellar entrance. Gill and his men were racing towards the small corral where they had left their horses.

Brett and Raina had better luck; they found the Mallin brothers' mounts where they had abandoned them, intent only on getting attention for Link's wound. One saddle on a smoke horse was smeared with blood, so that must have been Link's.

They mounted swiftly, Brett taking the one with the bloody saddle. The

237

stirrups were too short but he could lengthen them later — with any luck when they had dodged the posse. Raina settled on to the black mount she had been left with and saw the pack-mule, standing patiently with drooping head, a stubby wooden box roped to its back. She leaned out, grabbed the mule's reins and it followed the black readily enough as she dug in the spurs.

Brett was already astride his smoke, reloading the pistol, glad to see there was a rifle in the saddle scabbard. Then he glimpsed Raina leading the packmule and wondered what the hell she was doing? Until he saw the silhouette of the wooden box against the flames now spewing from the root cellar.

His teeth bared in a grin as he spurred after the girl. This was fall, October, but it could well be the Fourth of July a little later on this night.

⋆   ⋆   ⋆

'What went wrong?' Belle demanded as she worked on the bloody wound in Dean's left thigh. 'Damn you, Dean! We had it set up perfectly! Now both of them are on the loose.'

'Gill's gone after 'em,' he said wearily, not a little put out by the pain of his wounds.

Belle scoffed. 'With a posse of damn fools! They're townsmen. They'll never track Brett in the Whetstones, not with that Indian girl helping him!'

'Well, I can't damn well ride! Why don't you get on down to the pasture and grab half a dozen men and send 'em after Gill?'

She gave him a withering look. 'So! I have to be the one to get you out of trouble once more! I'm damn well sick and tired of it! I can see now why Pa was fed up with you!'

'Sounds just like you, sis. But think beyond your own inconvenience. Get Brett and the girl! Then you can worry about your own comfort, and with luck it'll be the *only* thing you'll

239

have to worry about.'

She stormed back into the house, muttering, and shortly afterwards saddled her sand-coloured mare and set off for the distant east pasture and the massed herds.

★ ★ ★

'We'd better make 'em think we're heading for the Whetstones,' Brett said as he and the girl climbed a winding trail. He was following her and the packmule with the box of dynamite.

'I'll do it. You know how to handle that stuff, you said. I know these trails and I can have them tied in a knot while you go to the dam.'

He nodded: an instant decision because it made sense. But he paused a moment: 'You get to high ground. Never mind anything else.'

She smiled faintly. 'I'll come to the dam.'

He started to tell her not to try but she was already spurring away.

240

★ ★ ★

'Hey! There's that damn squaw! Up on the high trail!'

It was Watty who yelled and Gill swore. 'That's it, Watty! Just a little louder so she can hear you and know we've spotted her!'

Watty looked sheepish and one of the other men said, 'She ain't even seen us, Sheriff. See? Still headin' towards the damn Whetstones!'

None of them liked the thought of going into those gloomy, dangerous ranges, especially at night.

'Well, might've known that's where they'd head,' growled the lawman. 'Let's get movin'.'

'Be lucky we get home before the middle of next week!' someone growled.

'Think of all the pay we'll make,' another voice said and Gill cursed them.

'Shut up and let's get up there. Remember, Brett's armed again.'

The men groaned and Barton Gill

241

grinned fiercely.

McCord's fine whiskey was wearing off, leaving him feeling less than happy, but it brightened him to know that these moaning bastards would be riding tight-assed, jumping at every shadow, earning every damn cent of their poss pay.

★ ★ ★

Brett was drenched with cold dam water, working out on the headgates' access platform below the mid-join where water spurted through. There was a lot of pressure behind it, and he felt the sting of it through his clothes. It streamed down his face, sloshed into his mouth, almost choking him as he fought for breath.

He had the dynamite slung across his shoulders on a short length of rope; there had been fourteen sticks in the box, half of them already primed with detonators and fuse caps. He had managed to prime the others without

242

fumbling too much and had already planted three bundles in a pattern he figured would burst open the gates. But he needed the fourth one to be sure and that was why he was clinging like a fly on to the front of the headgates as he worked out inch by inch, boots slipping on the wet wood, fingertips clawing into any crack within reach.

The first three were in reasonably dry areas, but this one he aimed to stuff into a gap where the join spurted water in a stream as thick as his arm. The dynamite would get wet but was still wrapped in its waxed paper, except for the top where he had pushed the detonator and fuse home.

He just hoped the fuse would burn quickly so the water didn't drown the bundle. He almost fell, decided this would have to do, and swung by the fingers of one hand, all his weight on the first joints, as he unslung the bundle. He reached up high as he could to jam it at the edge of the gap.

It stayed there but was trembling

with the surge of the water alongside. It seemed like he had been working for hours so he started back, unwinding the coiled fuse from his shoulders. On a dry spot, he rubbed his aching fingers, fumbled in his pocket for the small, waxed tin that contained his vestas. This had been in the box with the dynamite and he blessed the Mallin brothers for their professionalism. He dropped the first two matches, almost mashed the third one he held it so tightly. He scraped it over the roughened surface on the base of the tin.

He was blinded by the flare, holding the fuse with his teeth, letting a foot or so dangle down. He tried to hold the flame to the end with the inner core exposed, but the vesta died. He swore and repeated the whole process.

This time the inner core caught and began to sputter, smoking and making him cough. He held the fuse until a few inches had been consumed then let it dangle. He started back to the bank. Here he knelt and lit the fuses to the other three bundles; these were much shorter but, allowing for the time it took him to climb down, should reach the bundles pretty close to the time the other fuse set off the dynamite jammed between the head gates.

He swung aboard his mount and spurred away, riding up to the big pine tree above the dam, his heart hammering, as he looked for some sign of Raina. God, if she didn't get on to the high ground before the gates blew . . .

'I left the posse climbing into the ranges a good two miles away.' He jumped as she walked her sweating mount out of the brush. She smiled. 'You look jumpy. Were you — concerned for my safety, Brett?'

He looked at her soberly. 'What d'you think?'

'I — think it's very sweet of you.'

But she was never sure if he had heard her words, for just then there was a short but rapid series of thundering, ear-shattering explosions. The ground shook. Huge splinters and broken logs from the headgates thrummed through the air. Great chunks of concrete split and tumbled. There was a roar such as neither of them had heard before as a million gallons of water ejected in a massive, destructive arc, thundered down into the Arrowhead basin far below, annihilating tall trees and huge boulders, wrenching tons of earth from the mountain and carrying all the debris with it.

They watched in awe as the rushing flood obliterated the land, a foaming muddy wall rising, up — up — up . . . drowning everything as it advanced.

'That big herd . . . and the night-hawks . . . '

'They'll be OK. There're hogbacks and deep gulches between here and there. The water'll take the easiest way.' Brett indicated with his hand, chopping it downwards in a direct, arrow-straight line from where they sat their nervous mounts.

'That's right in line with Arrowhead!'

'Yeah.' He said it flatly, with just a

hint of satisfaction. 'On target.'

'I saw a rider making for the house as I swung over the crest. I think it was Belle. I hope she makes it in time.'

He looked at her levelly. 'Dean'll already be there with his wounded leg. They'll probably feel safe in the house.'

Raina drew in a sharp, deep breath. 'But — they won't be?'

Silently, he indicated the roaring flood and the direction it was taking; it advanced remorselessly across Arrowhead with the speed, force and destructive power of a hundred locomotives on the loose, thundering towards the distant ranch house, cannoning off highback rises, exploding in giant waves through and over gulches, smashing stands of timber flat. Nothing could remain standing in its path.

'You've kept your word to Danny,' she said slowly, and when he didn't answer, asked, 'What now?'

Still watching the flood, he said, 'I'm a drifter. How about you? You can't go

247

back to town as long as Barton Gill's sheriff.'

Her eyes were steady on his face. 'The tribe moved about frequently when I was a child. I often miss the constant changes of scenery, different people. You could call that 'drifting', I suppose.'

He smiled and looked back towards the house.

But there was only the brown surge of the floodwaters to be seen now, still spreading, all-encompassing, like some storm-tossed sea.

'Reckon we better be going.'

She ranged her horse alongside his and they rode back across the spur behind the ruins of the rapidly empty-ing dam, into the high country of the Whetstones.

Side by side.

THE END

We do hope that you have enjoyed reading this large print book.

Did you know that all of our titles are available for purchase?

We publish a wide range of high quality large print books including:
Romances, Mysteries, Classics
General Fiction
Non Fiction and Westerns

Special interest titles available in large print are:
The Little Oxford Dictionary
Music Book, Song Book
Hymn Book, Service Book

Also available from us courtesy of Oxford University Press:
Young Readers' Dictionary
(large print edition)
Young Readers' Thesaurus
(large print edition)

For further information or a free brochure, please contact us at:
Ulverscroft Large Print Books Ltd.,
The Green, Bradgate Road, Anstey,
Leicester, LE7 7FU, England.
Tel: (00 44) **0116 236 4325**
Fax: (00 44) **0116 234 0205**

Other titles in the
Linford Western Library:

APACHE RIFLES

Ethan Flagg

Brick Shaftoe hurries to the town of Brass Neck in New Mexico after he receives an urgent cable from his brother. The Apache chief, Manganellis, is being supplied with guns to terrorize the smaller ranchers. Then he finds that his brother has met with a fatal accident and he believes that this is no coincidence. Brick vows to discover the truth about what has been going on in Brass Neck ... no matter how rocky the road is along the way.